ANIMAL HEROES

Being the Histories of a CAT,
a DOG, a PIGEON, a LYNX,
Two WOLVES & a REINDEER
and *in Elucidation of the Same*
over 200 DRAWINGS

By ERNEST THOMPSON SETON,

Author of *Wild Animals I Have Known*, BIOGRAPHY of a *Grizzly*,
Two *Little Savages* etc. NATURALIST to
GOVT of MANITOBA

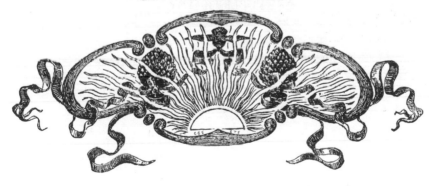

CREATIVE ARTS BOOK COMPANY · BERKELEY · 1987

CREATIVE ARTS BOOKS
ARE PUBLISHED BY
DONALD S. ELLIS

Cover design: Charles Fuhrman Design

ISBN 0-88739-055-2
Library of Congress No. 87-71143

NOTE FROM THE PUBLISHER:

In the process of assuming his family's true name, Seton was
known over a twenty-five year period as Ernest Evan Thompson,
Ernest Evan Thompson Seton, Ernest Thompson-Seton, Ernest
Seton-Thompson, Wolf Thompson, Wolf Seton and Chief Black
Wolf. In 1901 he took the legal name of Ernest Thompson Seton.

PRINTED IN THE UNITED STATES OF AMERICA

In this Book the designs for cover, title-
page, and general make-up were
done by Grace Gallatin Seton

A List of the Stories in this Book

And their Full-page Drawings

5

A List of the Stories in this Book

6

A List of the Stories in this Book

7

Note to Reader

A HERO is an individual of unusual gifts and achievements. Whether it be man or animal, this definition applies; and it is the histories of such that appeal to the imagination and to the hearts of those who hear them.

In this volume every one of the stories, though more or less composite, is founded on the actual life of a veritable animal hero. The most composite is the White Reindeer. This story I wrote by Utrovand in Norway during the summer of 1900, while the Reindeer herds grazed in sight on the near uplands.

The Lynx is founded on some of my own early experiences in the backwoods.

It is less than ten years since the 'Jack Warhorse' won his hero-crown. Thousands of "Kaskadoans" will remember him, and by

Note to Reader

the name *Warhorse* his coursing exploits are recorded in several daily papers.

The least composite is Arnaux. It is so nearly historical that several who knew the bird have supplied additional items of information.

The nest of the destroying Peregrines, with its owners and their young, is now to be seen in the American Museum of Natural History of New York. The Museum authorities inform me that Pigeon badges with the following numbers were found in the nest: 9970–S, 1696, ᴸ 63, 77, J. F. 52, Ex. 705, 6–1894, C 20900. Perhaps some Pigeon-lover may learn from these lines the fate of one or other wonderful flier that has long been recorded " never returned."

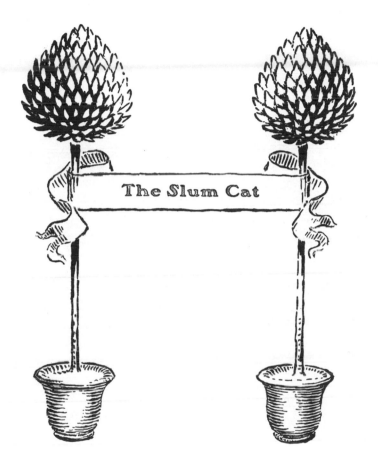

The Slum Cat

The Slum Cat

LIFE I

I

 "M-E-A-T! M-e-a-t!" came shrilling down Scrimper's Alley. Surely the Pied Piper of Hamelin was there, for it seemed that all the Cats in the neighborhood were running toward the sound, though the Dogs, it must be confessed, looked scornfully indifferent.

"Meat! Meat!" and louder; then the centre of attraction came in view—a rough, dirty little man with a push-cart; while straggling behind him were a score of Cats that joined in his cry with a sound nearly the same as his own. Every fifty yards, that is, as soon as a goodly throng of Cats was gathered, the push-cart stopped. The man with the magic voice took out of the box in his cart a skewer on which were pieces of strong-smelling boiled liver. With a long stick he pushed the pieces off. Each Cat seized on one, and wheeling, with a slight depression of the ears and a little tiger growl and glare, she rushed away with her prize to devour it in some safe retreat.

"Meat! Meat!" And still they came to get their portions. All were well known to the meat-man. There was Castiglione's Tiger; this was Jones's Black; here was Pralitsky's "Torkershell," and this was Madame Danton's White; there sneaked Blenkinshoff's Maltee, and that climbing on the barrow was Sawyer's old Orange Billy, an impudent fraud that never had had any financial backing,—all to be remembered and kept in account. This one's owner was sure pay, a dime a week; that one's doubtful. There was John Washee's Cat, that got only a small piece because John was in arrears. Then there was the saloon-keeper's collared and ribboned ratter, which got an extra lump because the 'barkeep' was liberal; and the rounds-

14

The Slum Cat

man's Cat, that brought no cash, but got unusual consideration because the meat-man did.
But there were others. A black Cat with a
white nose came rushing confidently with the
rest, only to be repulsed savagely. Alas! Pussy
did not understand. She had been a pensioner
of the barrow for months. Why this unkind
change? It was beyond her comprehension.
But the meat-man knew. Her mistress had
stopped payment. The meat-man kept no
books but his memory, and it never was at fault.

Outside this patrician 'four hundred' about
the barrow, were other Cats, keeping away from
the push-cart because they were not on the
list, the Social Register as it were, yet fascinated
by the heavenly smell and the faint possibility
of accidental good luck. Among these hangers-on was a thin gray Slummer, a homeless
Cat that lived by her wits—slab-sided and not
over-clean. One could see at a glance that she
was doing her duty by a family in some out-of-
the-way corner. She kept one eye on the barrow circle and the other on the possible Dogs.
She saw a score of happy Cats slink off with
their delicious 'daily' and their tiger-like air,

but no opening for her, till a big Tom of her own class sprang on a little pensioner with intent to rob. The victim dropped the meat to defend herself against the enemy, and before the 'all-powerful' could intervene, the gray Slummer saw her chance, seized the prize, and was gone.

HAPPY

She went through the hole in Menzie's side door and over the wall at the back, then sat down and devoured the lump of liver, licked her chops, felt absolutely happy, and set out by devious ways to the rubbish-yard, where, in the bottom of an old cracker-box, her family was awaiting her. A plaintive mewing reached her ears. She went at speed and reached the box to see a huge Black Tom-cat calmly destroying her brood. He was twice as big as she, but she went at him with all her strength, and he did as most animals will do when caught wrong-doing, he turned and ran away. Only one was left, a little thing like its mother, but of more pronounced color—gray with black spots, and a white touch on nose, ears, and tail-tip. There can be no question of the mother's grief for a few days; but that wore off, and all

her care was for the survivor. That benevo-
lence was as far as possible from the motives
of the murderous old Tom there can be no
doubt; but he proved a blessing in deep disguise, for both mother and Kit were visibly
bettered in a short time. The daily quest for
food continued. The meat-man rarely proved
a success, but the ash-cans were there, and if
they did not afford a meat-supply, at least they
were sure to produce potato-skins that could
be used to allay the gripe of hunger for another day.

One night the mother Cat smelt a wonderful
smell that came from the East River at the end
of the alley. A new smell always needs inves-
tigating, and when it is attractive as well as
new, there is but one course open. It led
Pussy to the docks a block away, and then
out on a wharf, away from any cover but the
night. A sudden noise, a growl and a rush,
were the first notice she had that she was cut
off by her old enemy, the Wharf Dog. There
was only one escape. She leaped from the
wharf to the vessel from which the smell came.
The Dog could not follow, so when the fish-

The Slum Cat

boat sailed in the morning Pussy unwillingly
went with her and was seen no more.

II

The Slum Kitten waited in vain for her mother.
The morning came and went. She became
very hungry. Toward evening a deep-laid instinct drove her forth to seek food. She slunk
out of the old box, and feeling her way silently
among the rubbish, she smelt everything that
seemed eatable, but without finding food. At
length she reached the wooden steps leading
down into Jap Malee's bird-store underground.
The door was open a little. She wandered
into a world of rank and curious smells and a
number of living things in cages all about her.
A negro was sitting idly on a box in a corner.
He saw the little stranger enter and watched it
curiously. It wandered past some Rabbits.
They paid no heed. It came to a wide-barred
cage in which was a Fox. The gentleman
with the bushy tail was in a far corner. He
crouched low; his eyes glowed. The Kitten
wandered, sniffing, up to the bars, put its head

18

The Slum Cat

in, sniffed again, then made toward the feed-pan, to be seized in a flash by the crouching Fox. It gave a frightened " mew," but a single shake cut that short and would have ended Kitty's nine lives at once, had not the negro come to the rescue. He had no weapon and could not get into the cage, but he spat with such copious vigor in the Fox's face that he dropped the Kitten and returned to the corner, there to sit blinking his eyes in sullen fear.

The negro pulled the Kitten out. The shake of the beast of prey seemed to have stunned the victim, really to have saved it much suffering. The Kitten seemed unharmed, but giddy. It tottered in a circle for a time, then slowly revived, and a few minutes later was purring in the negro's lap, apparently none the worse, when Jap Malee, the bird-man, came home.

Jap was not an Oriental; he was a full-blooded Cockney, but his eyes were such little accidental slits aslant in his round, flat face, that his first name was forgotten in the highly descriptive title of " Jap." He was not especially unkind to the birds and beasts whose sales were supposed to furnish his living, but his eye was on the main chance; he knew what he wanted. He did n't want the Slum Kitten.

The negro gave it all the food it could eat, then carried it to a distant block and dropped it in a neighboring iron-yard.

III

One full meal is as much as any one needs in two or three days, and under the influence of this stored-up heat and power, Kitty was very lively. She walked around the piled-up rubbish, cast curious glances on far-away Canary-birds in cages that hung from high windows; she peeped over fences, discovered a large Dog, got quietly down again, and presently finding a sheltered place in full sunlight, she lay down and slept for an hour. A slight 'sniff' awakened her, and before her stood a large Black Cat with glowing green eyes, and the thick neck and square jaws that distinguish the Tom; a scar marked his cheek, and his left ear was torn. His look was far from friendly; his ears moved backward a little,

20

The Slum Cat

his tail twitched, and a faint, deep sound came from his throat. The Kitten innocently walked toward him. She did not remember him. He rubbed the sides of his jaws on a post, and quietly, slowly turned and disappeared. The last that she saw of him was the end of his tail twitching from side to side; and the little Slummer had no idea that she had been as near death to-day, as she had been when she ventured into the fox-cage.

As night came on the Kitten began to feel hungry. She examined carefully the long invisible colored stream that the wind is made of. She selected the most interesting of its strands, and, nose-led, followed. In the corner of the iron-yard was a box of garbage. Among this she found something that answered fairly well for food; a bucket of water under a faucet offered a chance to quench her thirst.

The night was spent chiefly in prowling about and learning the main lines of the iron-yard. The next day she passed as before, sleeping in the sun. Thus the time wore on. Sometimes she found a good meal at the garbage-box, sometimes there was nothing. Once she found

the big Black Tom there, but discreetly withdrew before he saw her. The water-bucket
was usually at its place, or, failing that, there
were some muddy little pools on the stone
below. But the garbage-box was very unreliable. Once it left her for three days without
food. She searched along the high fence,
and seeing a small hole, crawled through that
and found herself in the open street. This
was a new world, but before she had ventured
far, there was a noisy, rumbling rush—a large
Dog came bounding, and Kitty had barely time
to run back into the hole in the fence. She was
dreadfully hungry, and glad to find some old
potato-peelings, which gave a little respite from
the hunger-pang. In the morning she did not
sleep, but prowled for food. Some Sparrows
chirruped in the yard. They were often there,
but now they were viewed with new eyes. The
steady pressure of hunger had roused the wild
hunter in the Kitten; those Sparrows were game
—were food. She crouched instinctively and
stalked from cover to cover, but the chirpers
were alert and flew in time. Not once, but
many times, she tried without result except to

The Slum Cat

she had a sense of ownership, and at once resented the presence of another small Cat. She approached this newcomer with threatening air. The two had got as far as snarling and spitting when a bucket of water from an upper window drenched them both and effectually cooled their wrath. They fled, the newcomer over the wall, Slum Kitty under the very box where she had been born. This whole back region appealed to her strongly, and here again she took up her abode. The yard had no more garbage food than the other and no water at all, but it was frequented by stray Rats and a few Mice of the finest quality; these were occasionally secured, and afforded not only a palatable meal, but were the cause of her winning a friend.

IV

Kitty was now fully grown. She was a striking-looking Cat of the tiger type. Her marks were black on a very pale gray, and the four beauty-spots of white on nose, ears, and tail-tip lent a certain distinction. She was very expert at getting a living, and yet she had some days of starvation and failed in her ambition of catching a Sparrow. She was quite alone, but a new force was coming into her life.

She was lying in the sun one August day, when a large Black Cat came walking along the top of a wall in her direction. She recognized him at once by his torn ear. She slunk into her box and hid. He picked his way gingerly, bounded lightly to a shed that was at the end of the yard, and was crossing the roof when a Yellow Cat rose up. The Black Tom glared and growled, so did the Yellow Tom. Their tails lashed from side to side. Strong throats growled and yowled. They approached each other with ears laid back, with muscles a-tense.

" Yow—yow—ow ! " said the Black One.

" Wow—w—w ! " was the slightly deeper answer.

" Ya—wow—wow—wow! " said the Black One, edging up half an inch nearer.

" Yow—w—w! " was the Yellow answer, as the blond Cat rose to full height and stepped with vast dignity a whole inch forward. " Yow —w! " and he went another inch, while his tail went swish, thump, from one side to the other.

" ' Yo-ow ! ' rumbled the Yellow One."

The Slum Cat

" Ya—wow—yow—w!" screamed the Black in a rising tone, and he backed the eighth of an inch, as he marked the broad, unshrinking breast before him.

Windows opened all around, human voices were heard, but the Cat scene went on.

" Yow—yow—ow !" rumbled the Yellow Peril, his voice deepening as the other's rose. " Yow! " and he advanced another step.

Now their noses were but three inches apart ; they stood sidewise, both ready to clinch, but each waiting for the other. They glared for three minutes in silence and like statues, except that each tail-tip was twisting.

The Yellow began again. " Yow—ow— ow!" in deep tone.

" Ya—a—a—a—a!" screamed the Black, with intent to strike terror by his yell; but he retreated one sixteenth of an inch. The Yellow walked up a long half-inch; their whiskers were mixing now; another advance, and their noses almost touched.

" Yo—w—w!" said Yellow, like a deep moan.

" Y—a—a—a—a—a—a !" screamed the

The Slum Cat

Black, but he retreated a thirty-second of an inch, and the Yellow Warrior closed and clinched like a demon.

Oh, how they rolled and bit and tore, especially the Yellow One!

How they pitched and gripped and hugged, but especially the Yellow One!

Over and over, sometimes one on top, sometimes another, but mostly the Yellow One; and farther till they rolled off the roof, amid cheers from all the windows. They lost not a second in that fall to the junk-yard; they tore and clawed all the way down, but especially the Yellow One. And when they struck the ground, still fighting, the one on top was chiefly the Yellow One; and before they separated both had had as much as they wanted, especially the Black One! He scaled a wall and, bleeding and growling, disappeared, while the news was passed from window to window that Cayley's Nig had been licked at last by Orange Billy.

Either the Yellow Cat was a very clever seeker, or else Slum Kitty did not hide very hard; but he discovered her among the boxes, and she made no attempt to get away, probably because she had witnessed the fight. There is nothing like success in warfare to win the female heart, and thereafter the Yellow Tom and Kitty became very good friends, not sharing each other's lives or food, — Cats do not do that way much, — but recognizing each other as entitled to special friendly privileges.

V

September had gone. October's shortening days were on when an event took place in the old cracker-box. If Orange Billy had come he would have seen five little Kittens curled up in the embrace of their mother, the little Slum Cat. It was a wonderful thing for her. She felt all the elation an animal mother can feel, all the delight, and she loved them and licked them with a tenderness that must have been a surprise to herself, had she had the power to think of such things.

She had added a joy to her joyless life, but she had also added a care and a heavy weight to her heavy load. All her strength was taken now to find food. The burden increased as the offspring grew up big enough to scramble about the boxes, which they did daily during her absence after they were six weeks old. That troubles go in flocks and luck in streaks, is well known in Slumland. Kitty had had three encounters with Dogs, and had been stoned by Malee's negro during a two days' starve. Then the tide turned. The very next morning she found a full milk-can without a lid, successfully robbed a barrow pensioner, and found a big fish-head, all within two hours. She had just returned with that perfect peace which comes only of a full stomach, when she saw a little brown creature in her junk-yard. Hunting memories came back in strength; she did n't know what it was, but she had killed and eaten several Mice, and this was evidently a big Mouse with bob-tail and large ears. Kitty stalked it with elaborate but unnecessary caution; the little Rabbit simply sat up and looked faintly amused. He did not try to run, and Kitty sprang on him and bore him off. As she was not hungry, she carried him to the cracker-box and dropped him among the Kittens. He

32

The Slum Cat

was not much hurt. He got over his fright, and since he could not get out of the box, he snuggled among the Kittens, and when they began to take their evening meal he very soon decided to join them. The old Cat was puzzled. The hunter instinct had been dominant, but absence of hunger had saved the Rabbit and given the maternal instinct a chance to appear. The result was that the Rabbit became a member of the family, and was thenceforth guarded and fed with the Kittens.

Two weeks went by. The Kittens romped much among the boxes during their mother's absence. The Rabbit could not get out of the box. Jap Malee, seeing the Kittens about the back yard, told the negro to shoot them. This he was doing one morning with a 22-calibre rifle. He had shot one after another and seen them drop from sight into the crannies of the lumber-pile, when the old Cat came running along the wall from the dock, carrying a small Wharf Rat. He had been ready to shoot her, too, but the sight of that Rat changed his plans: a rat-catching Cat was worthy to live. It happened to be the very first one she had ever caught, but it saved her life. She threaded the lumber-maze to the cracker-box and was probably puzzled to find that there were no Kittens to come at her call, and the Rabbit would not partake of the Rat. Pussy curled up to nurse the Rabbit, but she called from time to time to summon the Kittens. Guided by that call, the negro crawled quietly to the place, and peering down into the cracker-box, saw, to his intense surprise, that it contained the old Cat, a live Rabbit, and a dead Rat.

The mother Cat laid back her ears and snarled. The negro withdrew, but a minute later a board was dropped on the opening of the cracker-box, and the den with its tenants, dead and alive, was lifted into the bird-cellar.

"Say, boss, look a-hyar—hyar 's where de little Rabbit got to wot we lost. Yo' sho t'ought Ah stoled him for de 'tater-bake."

Kitty and Bunny were carefully put in a large wire cage and exhibited as a happy family till a few days later, when the Rabbit took sick and died.

Pussy had never been happy in the cage. She had enough to eat and drink, but she

The Slum Cat

craved her freedom—would likely have gotten 'death or liberty' now, but that during the four days' captivity she had so cleaned and slicked her fur that her unusual coloring was seen, and Jap decided to keep her.

LIFE II

VI

Jap Malee was as disreputable a little Cockney bantam as ever sold cheap Canary-birds in a cellar. He was extremely poor, and the negro lived with him because the 'Henglishman' was willing to share bed and board, and otherwise admit a perfect equality that few Americans conceded. Jap was perfectly honest according to his lights, but he had n't any lights; and it was well known that his chief revenue was derived from storing and restoring stolen Dogs and Cats. The half-dozen Canaries were mere blinds. Yet Jap believed in himself. " Hi tell you, Sammy, me boy, you 'll see me with 'orses of my own yet," he would say, when some trifling success inflated his dirty little chest. He was not without ambition, in a weak, flabby, once-in-a-while way, and he sometimes wished to be known as a fancier. Indeed, he had once gone the wild length of offering a Cat for exhibition at the Knickerbocker High Society Cat and Pet Show, with three not over-clear objects: first, to gratify his ambition; second, to secure the exhibitor's free pass; and, third, " well, you kneow, one 'as to kneow the valuable Cats, you kneow, when one goes a-catting." But this was a society show, the exhibitor had to be introduced, and his miserable alleged half-Persian was scornfully rejected. The 'Lost and Found' columns of the papers were the only ones of interest to Jap, but he had noticed and saved a clipping about 'breeding for fur.' This was stuck on the wall of his den, and under its influence he set about what seemed a cruel experiment with the Slum Cat. First, he soaked her dirty fur with stuff to kill the two or three kinds of creepers she wore; and, when it had done its work, he washed her thoroughly in soap and warm water, in spite of her teeth, claws, and yowls. Kitty was savagely indignant, but a warm and

The Slum Cat

happy glow spread over her as she dried off in a cage near the stove, and her fur began to fluff out with wonderful softness and whiteness. Jap and his assistant were much pleased with the result, and Kitty ought to have been. But this was preparatory: now for the experiment. " Nothing is so good for growing fur as plenty of oily food and continued exposure to cold weather," said the clipping. Winter was at hand, and Jap Malee put Kitty's cage out in the yard, protected only from the rain and the direct wind, and fed her with all the oil-cake and fish-heads she could eat. In a week a change began to show. She was rapidly getting fat and sleek—she had nothing to do but get fat and dress her fur. Her cage was kept clean, and nature responded to the chill weather and the oily food by making Kitty's coat thicker and glossier every day, so that by midwinter she was an unusually beautiful Cat in the fullest and finest of fur, with markings that were at least a rarity. Jap was much pleased with the result of the experiment, and as a very little success had a wonderful effect on him, he began to dream of the paths of glory. Why

not send the Slum Cat to the show now coming on? The failure of the year before made him more careful as to details. "'T won't do, ye kneow, Sammy, to henter 'er as a tramp Cat, ye kneow," he observed to his help; "but it kin be arranged to suit the Knickerbockers. Nothink like a good noime, ye kneow. Ye see now it had orter be 'Royal' somethink or other — nothink goes with the Knickerbockers like 'Royal' anythink. Now 'Royal Dick,' or 'Royal Sam,' 'ow's that? But 'owld on; them's Tom names. Oi say, Sammy, wot's the noime of that island where ye wuz born?"

"Analostan Island, sah, was my native vicinity, sah."

"Oi say, now, that's good, ye kneow. 'Royal Analostan,' by Jove! The onliest pedigreed 'Royal Analostan' in the 'ole sheow, ye kneow. Ain't that foine?" and they mingled their cackles.

"But we'll 'ave to 'ave a pedigree, ye kneow." So a very long fake pedigree on the recognized lines was prepared. One dark afternoon Sam, in a borrowed silk hat, delivered the Cat and the pedigree at the show door. The

The Slum Cat

darkey did the honors. He had been a Sixth Avenue barber, and he could put on more pomp and lofty hauteur in five minutes than Jap Malee could have displayed in a lifetime, and this, doubtless, was one reason for the respectful reception awarded the Royal Analostan at the Cat Show.

Jap was very proud to be an exhibitor; but he had all a Cockney's reverence for the upper class, and when on the opening day he went to the door, he was overpowered to see the array of carriages and silk hats. The gateman looked at him sharply, but passed him on his ticket, doubtless taking him for stable-boy to some exhibitor. The hall had velvet carpets before the long rows of cages. Jap, in his small cunning, was sneaking down the side rows, glancing at the Cats of all kinds, noting the blue ribbons and the reds, peering about but not daring to ask for his own exhibit, inly trembling to think what the gorgeous gathering of fashion would say if they discovered the trick he was playing on them. He had passed all around the outer aisles and seen many prize-winners, but no sign of Slum Kitty. The inner

aisles were more crowded. He picked his way
down them, but still no Kitty, and he decided
that it was a mistake; the judges had rejected
the Cat later. Never mind; he had his exhibitor's ticket, and now knew where several valuable Persians and Angoras were to be found.

In the middle of the centre aisle were the
high-class Cats. A great throng was there. The
passage was roped, and two policemen were in
place to keep the crowd moving. Jap wriggled
in among them; he was too short to see over,
and though the richly gowned folks shrunk from
his shabby old clothes, he could not get near;
but he gathered from the remarks that the gem
of the show was there.

"Oh, is n't she a beauty!" said one tall
woman.

"What distinction!" was the reply.

"One cannot mistake the air that comes only
from ages of the most refined surroundings."

"How I should like to own that superb
creature!"

"Such dignity—such repose!"

"She has an authentic pedigree nearly back
to the Pharaohs, I hear"; and poor, dirty little

The Slum Cat

Jap marvelled at his own cheek in sending his Slum Cat into such company.

" Excuse me, madame." The director of the show now appeared, edging his way through the crowd. " The artist of the ' Sporting Element ' is here, under orders to sketch the ' pearl of the show ' for immediate use. May I ask you to stand a little aside ? That 's it ; thank you."

" Oh, Mr. Director, cannot you persuade him to sell that beautiful creature ? "

" Hm, I don't know," was the reply. " I understand he is a man of ample means and not at all approachable ; but I 'll try, I 'll try, madame. He was quite unwilling to exhibit his treasure at all, so I understand from his butler. Here, you, keep out of the way," growled the director, as the shabby little man eagerly pushed between the artist and the blue-blooded Cat. But the disreputable one wanted to know where valuable Cats were to be found. He came near enough to get a glimpse of the cage, and there read a placard which announced that " The blue ribbon and *gold medal* of the Knickerbocker High Society Cat and Pet

Show" had been awarded to the "thorough-bred, pedigreed Royal Analostan, imported and exhibited by J. Malee, Esq., the well-known fancier. (Not for sale.)" Jap caught his breath and stared again. Yes, surely; there, high in a gilded cage, on velvet cushions, with four policemen for guards, her fur bright black and pale gray, her bluish eyes slightly closed, was his Slum Kitty, looking the picture of a Cat bored to death with a lot of fuss that she likes as little as she understands it.

VII

Jap Malee lingered around that cage, taking in the remarks, for hours—drinking a draught of glory such as he had never known in life before and rarely glimpsed in his dreams. But he saw that it would be wise for him to remain unknown; his "butler" must do all the business.

It was Slum Kitty who made that show a success. Each day her value went up in her owner's eyes. He did not know what prices had been given for Cats, and thought that he was

" There, . . . high on Velvet Cushions, . . . was his Slum Kitty."

The Slum Cat

touching a record pitch when his "butler"
gave the director authority to sell the Analostan
for one hundred dollars.

This is how it came about that the Slum Cat
found herself transferred from the show to a
Fifth Avenue mansion. She evinced a most
unaccountable wildness at first. Her objection
to petting, however, was explained on the
ground of her aristocratic dislike of familiar-
ity. Her retreat from the Lap-dog onto the
centre of the dinner-table was understood to
express a deep-rooted though mistaken idea of
avoiding a defiling touch. Her assaults on a
pet Canary were condoned for the reason that
in her native Orient she had been used to
despotic example. The patrician way in which
she would get the cover off a milk-can was
especially applauded. Her dislike of her silk-
lined basket, and her frequent dashes against
the plate-glass windows, were easily understood: the basket was too plain, and plate-
glass was not used in her royal home. Her
spotting of the carpet evidenced her Eastern
modes of thought. The failure of her several
attempts to catch Sparrows in the high-walled

back yard was new proof of the royal impotency of her bringing up; while her frequent wallowings in the garbage-can were understood to be the manifestation of a little pardonable high-born eccentricity. She was fed and pampered, shown and praised; but she was not happy. Kitty was homesick! She clawed at that blue ribbon round her neck till she got it off; she jumped against the plate-glass because that seemed the road to outside; she avoided people and Dogs because they had always proved hostile and cruel; and she would sit and gaze on the roofs and back yards at the other side of the window, wishing she could be among them for a change.

But she was strictly watched, was never allowed outside—so that all the happy garbage-can moments occurred while these receptacles of joy were indoors. One night in March, however, as they were set out a-row for the early scavenger, the Royal Analostan saw her chance, slipped out of the door, and was lost to view.

Of course there was a grand stir; but Pussy neither knew nor cared anything about that—

The Slum Cat

her one thought was to go home. It may
have been chance that took her back in the
direction of Gramercy Grange Hill, but she
did arrive there after sundry small adventures.
And now what? She was not at home, and she
had cut off her living. She was beginning to be
hungry, and yet she had a peculiar sense of
happiness. She cowered in a front garden for
some time. A raw east wind had been rising,
and now it came to her with a particularly
friendly message; man would have called it an
unpleasant smell of the docks, but to Pussy it
was welcome tidings from home. She trotted
down the long street due east, threading the
rails of front gardens, stopping like a statue for
an instant, or crossing the street in search of the
darkest side, and came at length to the docks
and to the water. But the place was strange.
She could go north or south. Something turned
her southward; and, dodging among docks and
Dogs, carts and Cats, crooked arms of the bay
and straight board fences, she got, in an hour
or two, among familiar scenes and smells; and,
before the sun came up, she had crawled back
weary and foot-sore through the same old hole

17

The Slum Cat

in the same old fence and over a wall to her
junk-yard back of the bird-cellar—yes, back
into the very cracker-box where she was born.

Oh, if the Fifth Avenue family could only
have seen her in her native Orient!

After a long rest she came quietly down
from the cracker-box toward the steps leading
to the cellar, engaged in her old-time pursuit
of seeking for eatables. The door opened, and
there stood the negro. He shouted to the
bird-man inside:

"Say, boss, come hyar. Ef dere ain't dat
dar Royal Ankalostan am comed back!"

Jap came in time to see the Cat jumping the
wall. They called loudly and in the most
seductive, wheedling tones: "Pussy, Pussy,
poor Pussy! Come, Pussy!" But Pussy was
not prepossessed in their favor, and disappeared
to forage in her old-time haunts.

The Royal Analostan had been a windfall
for Jap—had been the means of adding many
comforts to the cellar and several prisoners to
the cages. It was now of the utmost importance to recapture her majesty. Stale meat-
offal and other infallible lures were put out

48

The Slum Cat

till Pussy, urged by the reëstablished hunger-pinch, crept up to a large fish-head in a box-trap; the negro, in watching, pulled the string that dropped the lid, and, a minute later, the Analostan was once more among the prisoners in the cellar. Meanwhile Jap had been watching the 'Lost and Found' column. There it was, "$25 reward," etc. That night Mr. Malee's butler called at the Fifth Avenue mansion with the missing cat. "Mr. Malee's compliments, sah. De Royal Analostan had recurred in her recent proprietor's vicinity and residence, sah. Mr. Malee had pleasure in recuperating the Royal Analostan, sah." Of course Mr. Malee could not be rewarded, but the butler was open to any offer, and plainly showed that he expected the promised reward and something more.

Kitty was guarded very carefully after that; but so far from being disgusted with the old life of starving, and glad of her ease, she became wilder and more dissatisfied.

49

The Slum Cat

VIII

The spring was doing its New York best. The dirty little English Sparrows were tumbling over each other in their gutter brawls, Cats yowled all night in the areas, and the Fifth Avenue family were thinking of their country residence. They packed up, closed house, and moved off to their summer home, some fifty miles away, and Pussy, in a basket, went with them.

"Just what she needed: a change of air and scene to wean her away from her former owners and make her happy."

The basket was lifted into a Rumble-shaker. New sounds and passing smells were entered and left. A turn in the course was made. Then a roaring of many feet, more swinging of the basket; a short pause, another change of direction, then some clicks, some bangs, a long shrill whistle, and door-bells of a very big front door; a rumbling, a whizzing, an unpleasant smell, a hideous smell, a growing horrible, hateful choking smell, a deadly, griping, poisonous stench, with roaring that drowned poor

50

The Slum Cat

Kitty's yowls, and just as it neared the point where endurance ceased, there was relief. She heard clicks and clacks. There was light; there was air. Then a man's voice called, " All out for 125th Street," though of course to Kitty it was a mere human bellow. The roaring almost ceased—did cease. Later the rackety-bang was renewed with plenty of sounds and shakes, though not the poisonous gas; a long, hollow, booming roar with a pleasant dock smell was quickly passed, and then there was a succession of jolts, roars, jars, stops, clicks, clacks, smells, jumps, shakes, more smells, more shakes,—big shakes, little shakes, —gases, smokes, screeches, door-bells, tremblings, roars, thunders, and some new smells, raps, taps, heavings, rumblings, and more smells, but all without any of the feel that the direction is changed. When at last it stopped, the sun came twinkling through the basket-lid. The Royal Cat was lifted into a Rumble-shaker of the old familiar style, and, swerving aside from their past course, very soon the noises of its wheels were grittings and rattlings ; a new and horrible sound was added—the barking of

The Slum Cat

Dogs, big and little and dreadfully close. The basket was lifted, and Slum Kitty had reached her country home.

Every one was officiously kind. They wanted to please the Royal Cat, but somehow none of them did, except, possibly, the big, fat cook that Kitty discovered on wandering into the kitchen. This unctuous person smelt more like a slum than anything she had met for months, and the Royal Analostan was proportionately attracted. The cook, when she learned that fears were entertained about the Cat staying, said: "Shure, she 'd 'tind to thot; wanst a Cat licks her futs, shure she 's at home." So she deftly caught the unapproachable royalty in her apron, and committed the horrible sacrilege of greasing the soles of her feet with pot-grease. Of course Kitty resented it—she resented everything in the place; but on being set down she began to dress her paws and found evident satisfaction in that grease. She licked all four feet for an hour, and the cook triumphantly announced that now "shure she 'd be apt to shtay." And stay she did, but she showed a most surprising and disgusting preference for the kitchen, the cook, and the garbage-pail.

The family, though distressed by these distinguished peculiarities, were glad to see the Royal Analostan more contented and approachable. They gave her more liberty after a week or two. They guarded her from every menace. The Dogs were taught to respect her. No man or boy about the place would have dreamed of throwing a stone at the famous pedigreed Cat. She had all the food she wanted, but still she was not happy. She was hankering for many things, she scarcely knew what. She had everything—yes, but she wanted something else. Plenty to eat and drink—yes, but milk does not taste the same when you can go and drink all you want from a saucer; it has to be stolen out of a tin pail when you are belly-pinched with hunger and thirst, or it does not have the tang—it is n't milk.

Yes, there *was* a junk-yard back of the house and beside it and around it too, a big one, but it was everywhere poisoned and polluted with roses. The very Horses and Dogs had the wrong smells; the whole country round

The Slum Cat

was a repellent desert of lifeless, disgusting gardens and hay-fields, without a single tenement or smoke-stack in sight. How she did hate it all! There was only one sweet-smelling shrub in the whole horrible place, and that was in a neglected corner. She did enjoy nipping that and rolling in the leaves; it was a bright spot in the grounds; but the only one, for she had not found a rotten fish-head nor seen a genuine garbage-can since she came, and altogether it was the most unlovely, unattractive, unsmellable spot she had ever known. She would surely have gone that first night had she had the liberty. The liberty was weeks in coming, and, meanwhile, her affinity with the cook had developed as a bond to keep her; but one day after a summer of discontent a succession of things happened to stir anew the slum instinct of the royal prisoner.

A great bundle of stuff from the docks had reached the country mansion. What it contained was of little moment, but it was rich with a score of the most piquant and winsome of dock and slum smells. The chords of memory surely dwell in the nose, and Pussy's past was conjured up with dangerous force.

54

The Slum Cat

Next day the cook 'left' through some trouble
over this very bundle. It was the cutting of
cables, and that evening the youngest boy of
the house, a horrid little American with no
proper appreciation of royalty, was tying a tin
to the blue-blooded one's tail, doubtless in fur-
therance of some altruistic project, when Pussy
resented the liberty with a paw that wore five
big fish-hooks for the occasion. The howl of
downtrodden America roused America's mother. The deft and womanly blow that she
aimed with her book was miraculously avoided,
and Pussy took flight, up-stairs, of course. A
hunted Rat runs down-stairs, a hunted Dog
goes on the level, a hunted Cat runs up. She
hid in the garret, baffled discovery, and waited
till night came. Then, gliding down-stairs, she
tried each screen-door in turn, till she found one
unlatched, and escaped into the black August
night. Pitch-black to man's eyes, it was simply gray to her, and she glided through the disgusting shrubbery and flower-beds, took a final
nip at that one little bush that had been an attractive spot in the garden, and boldly took her
back track of the spring.

55

The Slum Cat

How could she take a back track that she never saw? There is in all animals some sense of direction. It is very low in man and very high in Horses, but Cats have a large gift, and this mysterious guide took her westward, not clearly and definitely, but with a general impulse that was made definite simply because the road was easy to travel. In an hour she had covered two miles and reached the Hudson River. Her nose had told her many times that the course was true. Smell after smell came back, just as a man after walking a mile in a strange street may not recall a single feature, but will remember, on seeing it again, "Why, yes, I saw that before." So Kitty's main guide was the sense of direction, but it was her nose that kept reassuring her, "Yes, now you are right—we passed this place last spring."

At the river was the railroad. She could not go on the water; she must go north or south. This was a case where her sense of direction was clear; it said, "Go south," and Kitty trotted down the foot-path between the iron rails and the fence.

The Slum Cat

LIFE III

IX

Cats can go very fast up a tree or over a wall, but when it comes to the long steady trot that reels off mile after mile, hour after hour, it is not the cat-hop, but the dog-trot, that counts. Although the travelling was good and the path direct, an hour had gone before two more miles were put between her and the Hades of roses. She was tired and a little foot-sore. She was thinking of rest when a Dog came running to the fence near by, and broke out into such a horrible barking close to her ear that Pussy leaped in terror. She ran as hard as she could down the path, at the same time watching to see if the Dog should succeed in passing the fence. No, not yet! but he ran close by it, growling horribly, while Pussy skipped along on the safe side. The barking of the Dog grew into a low rumble—a louder rumble and roaring—a terrifying thunder. A light shone. Kitty glanced back to see, not the Dog, but a

huge Black Thing with a blazing red eye coming on, yowling and spitting like a yard full of Cats. She put forth all her powers to run, made such time as she had never made before, but dared not leap the fence. She was running like a Dog, was flying, but all in vain; the monstrous pursuer overtook her, but missed her in the darkness, and hurried past to be lost in the night, while Kitty crouched gasping for breath, half a mile nearer home since that Dog began to bark.

This was her first encounter with the strange monster, strange to her eyes only; her nose seemed to know him and told her this was another landmark on the home trail. But Pussy lost much of her fear of his kind. She learned that they were very stupid and could not find her if she slipped quietly under a fence and lay still. Before morning she had encountered several of them, but escaped unharmed from all.

About sunrise she reached a nice little slum on her home trail, and was lucky enough to find several unsterilized eatables in an ash-heap. She spent the day around a stable where were two Dogs and a number of small boys, that

The Slum Cat

between them came near ending her career. It
was so very like home; but she had no idea
of staying there. She was driven by the old
craving, and next evening set out as before.
She had seen the one-eyed Thunder-rollers all
day going by, and was getting used to them,
so travelled steadily all that night. The next
day was spent in a barn where she caught a
Mouse, and the next night was like the last,
except that a Dog she encountered drove
her backward on her trail for a long way.
Several times she was misled by angling roads,
and wandered far astray, but in time she wandered back again to her general southward
course. The days were passed in skulking
under barns and hiding from Dogs and small
boys, and the nights in limping along the track,
for she was getting foot-sore; but on she went,
mile after mile, southward, ever southward—
Dogs, boys, Roarers, hunger—Dogs, boys,
Roarers, hunger—yet on and onward still she
went, and her nose from time to time cheered
her by confidently reporting, "There surely is
a smell we passed last spring."

59

The Slum Cat

X

So a week went by, and Pussy, dirty, ribbon-less, foot-sore, and weary, arrived at the Harlem Bridge. Though it was enveloped in delicious smells, she did not like the look of that bridge. For half the night she wandered up and down the shore without discovering any other means of going south, excepting some other bridges, or anything of interest except that here the men were as dangerous as the boys. Somehow she had to come back to it; not only its smells were familiar, but from time to time, when a One-eye ran over it, there was that peculiar rumbling roar that was a sensation in the springtime trip. The calm of the late night was abroad when she leaped to the timber stringer and glided out over the water. She had got less than a third of the way across when a thundering One-eye came roaring at her from the opposite end. She was much fright-ened, but knowing their stupidity and blind-ness, she dropped to a low side beam and there crouched in hiding. Of course the stupid Mon-

The Slum Cat

ster missed her and passed on, and all would have been well, but it turned back, or another just like it came suddenly spitting behind her. Pussy leaped to the long track and made for the home shore. She might have got there had not a third of the Red-eyed Terrors come screeching at her from that side. She was running her hardest, but was caught between two foes. There was nothing for it but a desperate leap from the timbers into—she did n't know what. Down, down, down—plop, splash, plunge into the deep water, not cold, for it was August, but oh, so horrible! She spluttered and coughed when she came to the top, glanced around to see if the Monsters were swimming after her, and struck out for shore. She had never learned to swim, and yet she swam, for the simple reason that a Cat's position and actions in swimming are the same as her position and actions in walking. She had fallen into a place she did not like; naturally she tried to *walk* out, and the result was that she swam ashore. Which shore ? The home-love never fails: the south side was the only shore for her, the one nearest home. She scrambled out all dripping

The Slum Cat

wet, up the muddy bank and through coal-piles
and dust-heaps, looking as black, dirty, and un-
royal as it was possible for a Cat to look.

Once the shock was over, the Royal-pedi-
greed Slummer began to feel better for the
plunge. A genial glow without from the bath,
a genial sense of triumph within, for had she
not outwitted three of the big Terrors?

Her nose, her memory, and her instinct of
direction inclined her to get on the track again;
but the place was infested with those Thunder-
rollers, and prudence led her to turn aside and
follow the river-bank with its musky home-
reminders; and thus she was spared the un-
speakable horrors of the tunnel.

She was over three days learning the manifold
dangers and complexities of the East River
docks. Once she got by mistake on a ferry-
boat and was carried over to Long Island; but
she took an early boat back. At length on the
third night she reached familiar ground, the place
she had passed the night of her first escape.
From that her course was sure and rapid. She
knew just where she was going and how to get
there. She knew even the more prominent

The Slum Cat

features in the Dog-scape now. She went faster, felt happier. In a little while surely she would be curled up in her native Orient — the old junk-yard. Another turn, and the block was in sight.

But—what! It was gone! Kitty could n't believe her eyes; but she must, for the sun was not yet up. There where once had stood or leaned or slouched or straggled the houses of the block, was a great broken wilderness of stone, lumber, and holes in the ground.

Kitty walked all around it. She knew by the bearings and by the local color of the pavement that she was in her home, that there had lived the bird-man, and there was the old junk-yard; but all were gone, completely gone, taking their familiar odors with them, and Pussy turned sick at heart in the utter hopelessness of the case. Her place-love was her master-mood. She had given up all to come to a home that no longer existed, and for once her sturdy little heart was cast down. She wandered over the silent heaps of rubbish and found neither consolation nor eatables. The ruin had taken in several of the blocks and reached back from the water. It was not a fire; Kitty had seen one of those things. This looked more like the work of a flock of the Red-eyed Monsters. Pussy knew nothing of the great bridge that was to rise from this very spot.

When the sun came up she sought for cover. An adjoining block still stood with little change, and the Royal Analostan retired to that. She knew some of its trails; but once there, was unpleasantly surprised to find the place swarming with Cats that, like herself, were driven from their old grounds, and when the garbage-cans came out there were several Slummers at each. It meant a famine in the land, and Pussy, after standing it a few days, was reduced to seeking her other home on Fifth Avenue. She got there to find it shut up and deserted. She waited about for a day; had an unpleasant experience with a big man in a blue coat, and next night returned to the crowded slum.

September and October wore away. Many of the Cats died of starvation or were too weak to escape their natural enemies. But Kitty, young and strong, still lived.

The Slum Cat

Great changes had come over the ruined blocks. Though silent on the night when she first saw them, they were crowded with noisy workmen all day. A tall building, well advanced on her arrival, was completed at the end of October, and Slum Kitty, driven by hunger, went sneaking up to a pail that a negro had set outside. The pail, unfortunately, was not for garbage; it was a new thing in that region: a scrubbing-pail. A sad disappointment, but it had a sense of comfort—there were traces of a familiar touch on the handle. While she was studying it, the negro elevator-boy came out again. In spite of his blue clothes, his odorous person confirmed the good impression of the handle. Kitty had retreated across the street. He gazed at her.

"Sho ef dat don't look like de Royal Ankalostan! Hyar, Pussy, Pussy, Pu-s-s-s-y! Co-o-o-o-m-e, Pu-u-s-s-sy, hyar! I 'spec's she 's sho hungry."

Hungry! She had n't had a real meal for months. The negro went into the building and reappeared with a portion of his own lunch.

65

The Slum Cat

"Hyar, Pussy, Puss, Puss, Puss!" It seemed very good, but Pussy had her doubts of the man. At length he laid the meat on the pavement, and went back to the door. Slum Kitty came forward very warily; sniffed at the meat, seized it, and fled like a little Tigress to eat her prize in peace.

LIFE IV

XI

This was the beginning of a new era. Pussy came to the door of the building now whenever pinched by hunger, and the good feeling for the negro grew. She had never understood that man before. He had always seemed hostile. Now he was her friend, the only one she had.

One week she had a streak of luck. Seven good meals on seven successive days; and right on the top of the last meal she found a juicy dead Rat, the genuine thing, a perfect windfall. She had never killed a full-grown Rat in all her lives, but seized the prize and ran off to hide it for future use. She was crossing the street

The Slum Cat

in front of the new building when an old enemy appeared,—the Wharf Dog,—and Kitty retreated, naturally enough, to the door where she had a friend. Just as she neared it, he opened the door for a well-dressed man to come out, and both saw the Cat with her prize.

"Hello! Look at that for a Cat!"

"Yes, sah," answered the negro. "Dat 's ma Cat, sah; she 's a terror on Rats, sah! hez 'em about cleaned up, sah; dat 's why she 's so thin."

"Well, don't let her starve," said the man with the air of the landlord. "Can't you feed her?"

"De liver meat-man comes reg'lar, sah; quatah dollar a week, sah," said the negro, fully realizing that he was entitled to the extra fifteen cents for "the idea."

"That 's all right. I 'll stand it."

XII

"M-e-a-t! M-e-a-t!" is heard the magnetic, cat-conjuring cry of the old liver-man, as his barrow is pushed up the glorified Scrimper's

The Slum Cat

Alley, and Cats come crowding, as of yore, to receive their due.

There are Cats black, white, yellow, and gray to be remembered, and, above all, there are owners to be remembered. As the barrow rounds the corner near the new building it makes a newly scheduled stop.

"Hyar, you, get out o' the road, you common trash," cries the liver-man, and he waves his wand to make way for the little gray Cat with blue eyes and white nose. She receives an unusually large portion, for Sam is wisely dividing the returns evenly; and Slum Kitty retreats with her 'daily' into shelter of the great building, to which she is regularly attached. She has entered into her fourth life with prospects of happiness never before dreamed of. Everything was against her at first; now everything seems to be coming her way. It is very doubtful that her mind was broadened by travel, but she knew what she wanted and she got it. She has achieved her long-time great ambition by catching, not *a* Sparrow, but two of them, while they were clinched in mortal combat in the gutter.

The Slum Cat

There is no reason to suppose that she ever caught another Rat; but the negro secures a dead one when he can, for purposes of exhibition, lest her pension be imperilled. The dead one is left in the hall till the proprietor comes; then it is apologetically swept away. "Well, drat dat Cat, sah; dat Royal Ankalostan blood, sah, is terrors on Rats."

She has had several broods since. The negro thinks the Yellow Tom is the father of some of them, and no doubt the negro is right.

He has sold her a number of times with a perfectly clear conscience, knowing quite well that it is only a question of a few days before the Royal Analostan comes back again. Doubtless he is saving the money for some honorable ambition. She has learned to tolerate the elevator, and even to ride up and down on it. The negro stoutly maintains that once, when she heard the meat-man, while she was on the top floor, she managed to press the button that called the elevator to take her down.

She is sleek and beautiful again. She is not only one of the four hundred that form the inner circle about the liver-barrow, but she is recognized as the star pensioner among them. The liver-man is positively respectful. Not even the cream-and-chicken fed Cat of the pawn-broker's wife has such a position as the Royal Analostan. But in spite of her prosperity, her social position, her royal name and fake pedigree, the greatest pleasure of her life is to slip out and go a-slumming in the gloaming, for now, as in her previous lives, she is at heart, and likely to be, nothing but a dirty little Slum Cat.

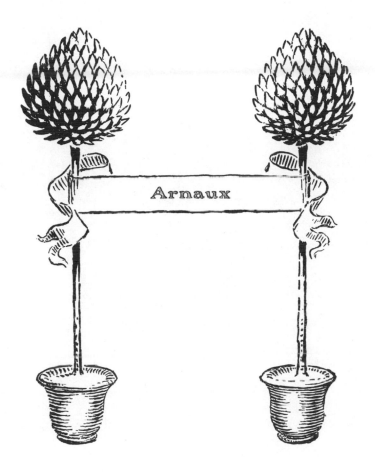

Arnaux

The Chronicle of a Homing Pigeon

I

WE passed through the side door of a big stable on West Nineteenth Street. The mild smell of the well-kept stalls was lost in the sweet odor of hay, as we mounted a ladder and entered the long garret. The south end was walled off, and the familiar "Coo-oo, cooooo-oo, ruk-at-a-coo," varied with the "whirr, whirr, whirr" of wings, informed us that we were at the pigeon-loft.

This was the home of a famous lot of birds, and to-day there was to be a race among fifty

73

of the youngsters.   The owner of the loft had asked me, as an unprejudiced outsider, to be judge in the contest.

It was a training race of the young birds. They had been taken out for short distances with their parents once or twice, then set free to return to the loft.   Now for the first time they were to be flown without the old ones. The point of start, Elizabeth, N. J., was a long journey for their first unaided attempt.   " But then," the trainer remarked, "that 's how we weed out the fools; only the best birds make it, and that 's all we want back."

There was another side to the flight.   It was to be a race among those that did return. Each of the men about the loft as well as several neighboring fanciers were interested in one or other of the Homers.   They made up a purse for the winner, and on me was to devolve the important duty of deciding which should take the stakes.   Not the first bird *back*, but the first bird *into the loft*, was to win, for one that returns to his neighborhood merely, without immediately reporting at home, is of little use as a letter-carrier.

74

Arnaux

The Homing Pigeon used to be called the
Carrier because it carried messages, but here
I found that name restricted to the show
bird, the creature with absurdly developed
wattles; the one that carries the messages is
now called the Homer, or Homing Pigeon—
the bird that always comes home. These Pigeons are not of any special color, nor have they
any of the fancy adornments of the kind that
figure in Bird shows. They are not bred for
style, but for speed and for their mental gifts.
They must be true to their home, able to return to it without fail. The sense of direction
is now believed to be located in the bony laby-
rinth of the ear. There is no creature with
finer sense of locality and direction than a good
Homer, and the only visible proofs of it are
the great bulge on each side of the head over
the ears, and the superb wings that complete
his equipment to obey the noble impulse of
home-love. Now the mental and physical
equipments of the last lot of young birds were
to be put to test.

Although there were plenty of witnesses, I
thought it best to close all but one of the pig-

75

eon-doors and stand ready to shut that behind
the first arrival.

I shall never forget the sensations of that
day. I had been warned: "They start at 12;
they should be here at 12:30; but look out,
they come like a whirlwind. You hardly see
them till they 're in."

We were ranged along the inside of the loft,
each with an eye to a crack or a partly closed
pigeon-door, anxiously scanning the southwest-
ern horizon, when one shouted: "Look out—
here they come!" Like a white cloud they
burst into view, low skimming over the city
roofs, around a great chimney pile, and in two
seconds after first being seen they were back.
The flash of white, the rush of pinions, were all
so sudden, so short, that, though preparing, I
was unprepared. I was at the only open door.
A whistling arrow of blue shot in, lashed my
face with its pinions, and passed. I had hardly
time to drop the little door, as a yell burst
from the men, "Arnaux! Arnaux! I told you
he would. Oh, he 's a darling; only three
months old and a winner—he 's a little darling!" and Arnaux's owner danced, more

Arnaux

for joy in his bird than in the purse he had won.

The men sat or kneeled and watched him in positive reverence as he gulped a quantity of water, then turned to the food-trough.

"Look at that eye, those wings, and did you ever see such a breast? Oh, but he 's the real grit!" so his owner prattled to the silent ones whose birds had been defeated.

That was the first of Arnaux's exploits. Best of fifty birds from a good loft, his future was bright with promise.

He was invested with the silver anklet of the Sacred Order of the High Homer. It bore his number, 2590 C, a number which to-day means much to all men in the world of the Homing Pigeon.

In that trial flight from Elizabeth only forty birds had returned. It is usually so. Some were weak and got left behind, some were foolish and strayed. By this simple process of flight selection the pigeon-owners keep improving their stock. Of the ten, five were seen no more, but five returned later that day, not all at once, but straggling in; the last of the

loiterers was a big, lubberly Blue Pigeon. The
man in the loft at the time called: "Here
comes that old sap-headed Blue that Jakey was
betting on. I did n't suppose he would come
back, and I did n't care, neither, for it 's my
belief he has a streak of Pouter."

The Big Blue, also called "Corner-box" from
the nest where he was hatched, had shown remarkable vigor from the first. Though all
were about the same age, he had grown faster,
was bigger, and incidentally handsomer, though
the fanciers cared little for that. He seemed
fully aware of his importance, and early showed
a disposition to bully his smaller cousins. His
owner prophesied great things of him, but Billy,
the stable-man, had grave doubts over the length
of his neck, the bigness of his crop, his carriage,
and his over-size. "A bird can't make time
pushing a bag of wind ahead of him. Them
long legs is dead weight, an' a neck like that
ain't got no gimp in it," Billy would grunt dis-
paragingly as he cleaned out the loft of a
morning.

Arnaux

II

The training of the birds went on after this at regular times. The distance from home, of the start, was "jumped" twenty-five or thirty miles farther each day, and its direction changed till the Homers knew the country for one hundred and fifty miles around New York. The original fifty birds dwindled to twenty, for the rigid process weeds out not only the weak and ill-equipped, but those also who may have temporary ailments or accidents, or who may make the mistake of over-eating at the start. There were many fine birds in that flight, broadbreasted, bright-eyed, long-winged creatures, formed for swiftest flight, for high unconscious emprise, for these were destined to be messengers in the service of man in times of serious need. Their colors were mostly white, blue, or brown. They wore no uniform, but each and all of the chosen remnant had the brilliant eye and the bulging ears of the finest Homer blood; and, best and choicest of all, nearly always first among them was little Arnaux. He

had not much to distinguish him when at rest,
for now all of the band had the silver anklet, but
in the air it was that Arnaux showed his make,
and when the opening of the hamper gave the
order "Start," it was Arnaux that first got
under way, soared to the height deemed needful to exclude all local influence, divined the
road to home, and took it, pausing not for
food, drink, or company.

Notwithstanding Billy's evil forecasts, the
Big Blue of the Corner-box was one of the
chosen twenty.   Often he was late in returning; he never was first, and sometimes when
he came back hours behind the rest, it was
plain that he was neither hungry nor thirsty,
sure signs that he was a loiterer by the way.
Still he had come back; and now he wore on
his ankle, like the rest, the sacred badge and a
number from the roll of possible fame.   Billy
despised him, set him in poor contrast with
Arnaux, but his owner would reply: " Give
him a chance; 'soon ripe, soon rotten,' an' I
always notice the best bird is the slowest to
show up at first."

Before a year little Arnaux had made a rec-

Arnaux

ord.   The hardest of all work is over the sea,
for there is no chance of aid from landmarks;
and the hardest of all times at sea is in fog, for
then even the sun is blotted out and there is
nothing whatever for guidance.   With memory, sight, and hearing unavailable, the Homer
has one thing left, and herein is his great
strength, the inborn sense of direction.   There
is only one thing that can destroy this, and
that is *fear*, hence the necessity of a stout little
heart between those noble wings.

Arnaux, with two of his order, in course of
training, had been shipped on an ocean steamer
bound for Europe.   They were to be released
out of sight of land, but a heavy fog set in and
forbade the start.   The steamer took them onward, the intention being to send them back with
the next vessel.   When ten hours out the engine
broke down, the fog settled dense over the sea,
and the vessel was adrift and helpless as a log.
She could only whistle for assistance, and so
far as results were concerned, the captain
might as well have wigwagged.   Then the
Pigeons were thought of.   Starback, 2592 C,
was first selected.   A message for help was

Arnaux

written on waterproof paper, rolled up, and lashed to his tail-feathers on the under side. He was thrown into the air and disappeared. Half an hour later, a second, the Big Blue Corner-box, 2600 C, was freighted with a letter. He flew up, but almost immediately returned and alighted on the rigging. He was a picture of pigeon fear; nothing could induce him to leave the ship. He was so terrorized that he was easily caught and ignominiously thrust back into the coop.

Now the third was brought out, a small, chunky bird. The shipmen did not know him, but they noted down from his anklet his name and number, Arnaux, 2590 C. It meant nothing to them. But the officer who held him noted that his heart did not beat so wildly as that of the last bird. The message was taken from the Big Blue. It ran:

10 A.M., Tuesday.

We broke our shaft two hundred and ten miles out from New York; we are drifting helplessly in the fog. Send out a tug as soon as possible. We are whistling one long, followed at once by one short, every sixty seconds.

(Signed)   THE CAPTAIN.

" He circled out of sight above the Ship."

Arnaux

This was rolled up, wrapped in waterproof
film, addressed to the Steamship Company, and
lashed to the under side of Arnaux's middle
tail-feather.

When thrown into the air, he circled round
the ship, then round again higher, then again
higher in a wider circle, and he was lost to
view; and still higher till quite out of sight and
feeling of the ship. Shut out from the use of
all his senses now but one, he gave himself up
to that. Strong in him it was, and untrammelled
of that murderous despot *Fear*. True as a
needle to the Pole went Arnaux now, no hesita-
tion, no doubts; within one minute of leaving
the coop he was speeding straight as a ray of
light for the loft where he was born, the only
place on earth where he could be made content.

That afternoon Billy was on duty when the
whistle of fast wings was heard; a blue Flyer
flashed into the loft and made for the water-
trough. He was gulping down mouthful after
mouthful, when Billy gasped: "Why, Arnaux,
it 's you, you beauty." Then, with the quick
habit of the pigeon-man, he pulled out his
watch and marked the time, 2:40 P.M. A

glance showed the tie string on the tail. He shut the door and dropped the catching-net quickly over Arnaux's head. A moment later he had the roll in his hand; in two minutes he was speeding to the office of the Company, for there was a fat tip in view. There he learned that Arnaux had made the two hundred and ten miles in fog, over sea, in four hours and forty minutes, and within one hour the needful help had set out for the unfortunate steamer.

Two hundred and ten miles in fog over sea in four hours and forty minutes! This was a noble record. It was duly inscribed in the rolls of the Homing Club. Arnaux was held while the secretary, with rubber stamp and indelible ink, printed on a snowy primary of his right wing the record of the feat, with the date and reference number.

Starback, the second bird, never was heard of again. No doubt he perished at sea.

Blue Corner-box came back on the tug.

Arnaux

III

That was Arnaux's first public record; but others came fast, and several curious scenes were enacted in that old pigeon-loft with Arnaux as the central figure. One day a carriage drove up to the stable; a white-haired gentleman got out, climbed the dusty stairs, and sat all morning in the loft with Billy. Peering from his gold-rimmed glasses, first at a lot of papers, next across the roofs of the city, waiting, watching, for what? News from a little place not forty miles away—news of greatest weight to him, tidings that would make or break him, tidings that must reach him before it could be telegraphed: a telegram meant at least an hour's delay at each end. What was faster than that for forty miles? In those days there was but one thing—a high-class Homer. Money would count for nothing if he could win. The best, the very best at any price he must have, and Arnaux, with seven indelible records on his pinions, was the chosen messenger. An hour went by, another, and a third was begun, when with

whistle of wings, the blue meteor flashed into
the loft. Billy slammed the door and caught
him. Deftly he snipped the threads and handed
the roll to the banker. The old man turned
deathly pale, fumbled it open, then his color
came back. " Thank God !" he gasped, and
then went speeding to his Board meeting, master
of the situation. Little Arnaux had saved him.

The banker wanted to buy the Homer, feeling in a vague way that he ought to honor
and cherish him; but Billy was very clear
about it. " What 's the good ? You can't buy
a Homer's heart. You could keep him a
prisoner, that 's all; but nothing on earth could
make him forsake the old loft where he was
hatched." So Arnaux stayed at 211 West
Nineteenth Street. But the banker did not
forget.

There is in our country a class of miscreants
who think a flying Pigeon is fair game, because
it is probably far from home, or they shoot him
because it is hard to fix the crime. Many a
noble Homer, speeding with a life or death
message, has been shot down by one of these
wretches and remorselessly made into a pot-pie.

Arnaux

Arnaux's brother Arnolf, with three fine records on his wings, was thus murdered in the act of bearing a hasty summons for the doctor. As he fell dying at the gunner's feet, his superb wings spread out displayed his list of victories. The silver badge on his leg was there, and the gunner was smitten with remorse. He had the message sent on ; he returned the dead bird to the Homing Club, saying that he " found it." The owner came to see him ; the gunner broke down under cross-examination, and was forced to admit that he himself had shot the Homer, but did so in behalf of a poor sick neighbor who craved a pigeon-pie.

There were tears in the wrath of the pigeon-man. " My bird, my beautiful Arnolf, twenty times has he brought vital messages, three times has he made records, twice has he saved human lives, and you 'd shoot him for a pot-pie. I could punish you under the law, but I have no heart for such a poor revenge. I only ask you this, if ever again you have a sick neighbor who wants a pigeon-pie, come, we 'll freely supply him with pie-breed squabs ; but if you have a trace of manhood about you, you will never,

never again shoot, or allow others to shoot, our noble and priceless messengers."

This took place while the banker was in touch with the loft, while his heart was warm for the Pigeons. He was a man of influence, and the Pigeon Protective legislation at Albany was the immediate fruit of Arnaux's exploit.

IV

Billy had never liked the Corner-box Blue (2600 C); notwithstanding the fact that he still continued in the ranks of the Silver Badge, Billy believed he was poor stuff. The steamer incident seemed to prove him a coward; he certainly was a bully.

One morning when Billy went in there was a row, two Pigeons, a large and a small, alternately clinching and sparring all over the floor, feathers flying, dust and commotion everywhere. As soon as they were separated Billy found that the little one was Arnaux and the big one was the Corner-box Blue. Arnaux had made a good fight, but was overmatched, for the Big Blue was half as heavy again.

Arnaux

Soon it was very clear what they had fought over—a pretty little lady Pigeon of the bluest Homing blood. The Big Blue cock had kept up a state of bad feeling by his bullying, but it was the Little Lady that had made them close in mortal combat. Billy had no authority to wring the Big Blue's neck, but he interfered as far as he could in behalf of his favorite Arnaux.

Pigeon marriages are arranged somewhat like those of mankind. Propinquity is the first thing: force the pair together for a time and let nature take its course. So Billy locked Arnaux and the Little Lady up together in a separate apartment for two weeks, and to make doubly sure he locked Big Blue up with an Available Lady in another apartment for two weeks.

Things turned out just as was expected. The Little Lady surrendered to Arnaux and the Available Lady to the Big Blue. Two nests were begun and everything shaped for a "lived happily ever after." But the Big Blue was very big and handsome. He could blow out his crop and strut in the sun and make rainbows

Arnaux

all round his neck in a way that might turn the heart of the staidest Homerine.

Arnaux, though sturdily built, was small and except for his brilliant eyes, not especially good-looking. Moreover, he was often away on important business, and the Big Blue had nothing to do but stay around the loft and display his unlettered wings.

It is the custom of moralists to point to the lower animals, and especially to the Pigeon, for examples of love and constancy, and properly so, but, alas! there are exceptions. Vice is not by any means limited to the human race.

Arnaux's wife had been deeply impressed with the Big Blue, at the outset, and at length while her spouse was absent the dreadful thing took place.

Arnaux returned from Boston one day to find that the Big Blue, while he retained his own Available Lady in the corner-box, had also annexed the box and wife that belonged to himself, and a desperate battle followed. The only spectators were the two wives, but they maintained an indifferent aloofness. Arnaux fought with his famous wings, but they were

Arnaux

none the better weapons because they now bore twenty records. His beak and feet were small, as became his blood, and his stout little heart could not make up for his lack of weight. The battle went against him. His wife sat unconcernedly in the nest, as though it were not her affair, and Arnaux might have been killed but for the timely arrival of Billy. He was angry enough to wring the Blue bird's neck, but the bully escaped from the loft in time. Billy took tender care of Arnaux for a few days. At the end of a week he was well again, and in ten days he was once more on the road. Meanwhile he had evidently forgiven his faithless wife, for, without any apparent feeling, he took up his nesting as before. That month he made two new records. He brought a message ten miles in eight minutes, and he came from Boston in four hours. Every moment of the way he had been impelled by the master-passion of home-love. But it was a poor home-coming if his wife figured at all in his thoughts, for he found her again flirting with the Big Blue cock. Tired as he was, the duel was renewed, and again would have been to a finish but for Billy's interference. He separated the fighters, then shut the Blue cock up in a coop, determined to get rid of him in some way. Meanwhile the " Any Age Sweepstakes " handicap from Chicago to New York was on, a race of nine hundred miles. Arnaux had been entered six months before. His forfeit-money was up, and notwithstanding his domestic complications, his friends felt that he must not fail to appear.

The birds were sent by train to Chicago, to be liberated at intervals there according to their handicap, and last of the start was Arnaux. They lost no time, and outside of Chicago several of these prime Flyers joined by common impulse into a racing flock that went through air on the same invisible track. A Homer may make a straight line when following his general sense of direction, but when following a familiar back track he sticks to the well-remembered landmarks. Most of the birds had been trained by way of Columbus and Buffalo. Arnaux knew the Columbus route, but also he knew that by Detroit, and after leaving Lake Michigan, he took the straight line for Detroit. Thus he caught up on his handicap and had the advantage of

Arnaux

many miles. Detroit, Buffalo, Rochester, with their familiar towers and chimneys, faded behind him, and Syracuse was near at hand. It was now late afternoon ; six hundred miles in twelve hours he had flown and was undoubtedly leading the race ; but the usual thirst of the Flyer had attacked him. Skimming over the city roofs, he saw a loft of Pigeons, and descending from his high course in two or three great circles, he followed the ingoing Birds to the loft and drank greedily at the water-trough, as he had often done before, and as every pigeon-lover hospitably expects the messengers to do. The owner of the loft was there and noted the strange Bird. He stepped quietly to where he could inspect him. One of his own Pigeons made momentary opposition to the stranger, and Arnaux, sparring sidewise with an open wing in Pigeon style, displayed the long array of printed records. The man was a fancier. His interest was aroused ; he pulled the string that shut the flying door, and in a few minutes Arnaux was his prisoner.

The robber spread the much-inscribed wings, read record after record, and glancing at

95

Arnaux

the silver badge—it should have been gold—
he read his name—Arnaux; then exclaimed:
" Arnaux! Arnaux! Oh, I 've heard of you,
you little beauty, and it 's glad I am to trap you."
He snipped the message from his tail, un-
rolled it, and read : " Arnaux left Chicago this
morning at 4 A.M., scratched in the Any Age
Sweepstakes for New York."

" Six hundred miles in twelve hours! By the
powers, that 's a record-breaker." And the
pigeon-stealer gently, almost reverently, put
the fluttering Bird safely into a padded cage.
" Well," he added, " I know it 's no use trying
to make you stay, but I can breed from you
and have some of your strain."

So Arnaux was shut up in a large and com-
fortable loft with several other prisoners. The
man, though a thief, was a lover of Homers;
he gave his captive everything that could
insure his comfort and safety. For three
months he left him in that loft. At first Arnaux did nothing all day but walk up and
down the wire screen, looking high and low
for means of escape; but in the fourth month
he seemed to have abandoned the attempt, and

Arnaux

the watchful jailer began the second part of
his scheme. He introduced a coy young lady
Pigeon. But it did not seem to answer; Arnaux was not even civil to her. After a time the
jailer removed the female, and Arnaux was left
in solitary confinement for a month. Now a
different female was brought in, but with no
better luck; and thus it went on—for a year
different charmers were introduced. Arnaux
either violently repelled them or was scornfully
indifferent, and at times the old longing to get
away, came back with twofold power, so that
he darted up and down the wire front or
dashed with all his force against it.

When the storied feathers of his wings began their annual moult, his jailer saved them
as precious things, and as each new feather
came he reproduced on it the record of its
owner's fame.

Two years went slowly by, and the jailer
had put Arnaux in a new loft and brought in
another lady Pigeon. By chance she closely
resembled the faithless one at home. Arnaux
actually heeded the newcomer. Once the
jailer thought he saw his famous prisoner pay-

97

Arnaux

ing some slight attention to the charmer, and, yes, he surely saw her preparing a nest. Then assuming that they had reached a full understanding, the jailer, for the first time, opened the outlet, and Arnaux was free. Did he hang around in doubt? Did he hesitate? No, not for one moment. As soon as the drop of the door left open the way, he shot through, he spread those wonderful blazoned wings, and, with no second thought for the latest Circe, sprang from the hated prison loft—away and away.

V

We have no means of looking into the Pigeon's mind; we may go wrong in conjuring up for it deep thoughts of love and welcome home; but we are safe in this, we cannot too strongly paint, we cannot too highly praise and glorify that wonderful God-implanted, mankind-fostered home-love that glows unquenchably in this noble bird. Call it what you like, a mere instinct deliberately constructed by man for his selfish ends, explain it away if you will, dissect it, misname it, and it still is there, in over-

Arnaux

whelming, imperishable master-power, as long as the brave little heart and wings can beat.

Home, home, sweet home! Never had mankind a stronger love of home than Arnaux. The trials and sorrows of the old pigeon-loft were forgotten in that all-dominating force of his nature. Not years of prison bars, not later loves, nor fear of death, could down its power; and Arnaux, had the gift of song been his, must surely have sung as sings a hero in his highest joy, when sprang he from the 'lighting board, up-circling free, soaring, drawn by the only impulse that those glorious wings would honor,—up, up, in widening, heightening circles of ashy blue in the blue, flashing those many-lettered wings of white, till they seemed like jets of fire—up and on, driven by that home-love, faithful to his only home and to his faithless mate; closing his eyes, they say; closing his ears, they tell; shutting his mind,—we all believe,—to nearer things, to two years of his life, to one half of his prime, but soaring in the blue, retiring, as a saint might do, into his inner self, giving himself up to that inmost guide. He was the captain of the ship, but the pilot, the chart and compass, all, were that deep-implanted instinct. One thousand feet above the trees the inscrutable whisper came, and Arnaux in arrowy swiftness now was pointing for the south-southeast. The little flashes of white fire on each side were lost in the low sky, and the reverent robber of Syracuse saw Arnaux nevermore.

The fast express was steaming down the valley. It was far ahead, but Arnaux overtook and passed it, as the flying wild Duck passes the swimming Muskrat. High in the valleys he went, low over the hills of Chenango, where the pines were combing the breezes.

Out from his oak-tree eyrie a Hawk came wheeling and sailing, silent, for he had marked the Flyer, and meant him for his prey. Arnaux turned neither right nor left, nor raised nor lowered his flight, nor lost a wing-beat. The Hawk was in waiting in the gap ahead, and Arnaux passed him, even as a Deer in his prime may pass by a Bear in his pathway. Home! home! was the only burning thought, the blinding impulse.

Beat, beat, beat, those flashing pinions went

Arnaux

with speed unslacked on the now familiar road. In an hour the Catskills were at hand. In two hours he was passing over them. Old friendly places, swiftly coming now, lent more force to his wings. Home! home! was the silent song that his heart was singing. Like the traveller dying of thirst, that sees the palm-trees far ahead, his brilliant eyes took in the distant smoke of Manhattan.

Out from the crest of the Catskills there launched a Falcon. Swiftest of the race of rapine, proud of his strength, proud of his wings, he rejoiced in a worthy prey. Many and many a Pigeon had been borne to his nest, and riding the wind he came, swooping, reserving his strength, awaiting the proper time. Oh, how well he knew the very moment! Down, down like a flashing javelin; no wild Duck, no Hawk could elude him, for this was a Falcon. Turn back now, O Homer, and save yourself; go round the dangerous hills. Did he turn? Not a whit! for this was Arnaux. Home! home! home! was his only thought. To meet the danger, he merely added to his speed; and the Peregrine stooped; stooped at what?—a

Arnaux

flashing of color, a twinkling of whiteness—and
went back empty. While Arnaux cleft the air
of the valley as a stone from a sling, to be lost—
a white-winged bird—a spot with flashing halo
—and, quickly, a speck in the offing. On down
the dear valley of Hudson, the well-known
highway; for two years he had not seen it!
Now he dropped low as the noon breeze came
north and ruffled the river below him. Home!
home! home! and the towers of a city are
coming in view! Home! home! past the
great spider-bridge of Poughkeepsie, skimming,
skirting the river-banks. Low now by the
bank as the wind arose. Low, alas! too low!
What fiend was it tempted a gunner in June to
lurk on that hill by the margin? what devil
directed his gaze to the twinkling of white that
came from the blue to the northward? Oh,
Arnaux, Arnaux, skimming low, forget not the
gunner of old! Too low, too low you are clearing that hill. Too low—*too late!* Flash—
bang! and the death-hail has reached him;
reached, maimed, but not downed him. Out
of the flashing pinions broken feathers printed
with records went fluttering earthward. The

Arnaux

"naught" of his sea record was gone. Not two hundred and ten, but twenty-one miles it now read. Oh, shameful pillage! A dark stain appeared on his bosom, but Arnaux kept on. Home, home, homeward bound. The danger was past in an instant. Home, homeward he steered straight as before, but the wonderful speed was diminished; not a mile a minute now; and the wind made undue sounds in his tattered pinions. The stain in his breast told of broken force; but on, straight on, he flew. Home, home was in sight, and the pain in his breast was forgotten. The tall towers of the city were in clear view of his far-seeing eye as he skimmed by the high cliffs of Jersey. On, on—the pinion might flag, the eye might darken, but the home-love was stronger and stronger.

Under the tall Palisades, to be screened from the wind, he passed, over the sparkling water, over the trees, under the Peregrines' eyrie, under the pirates' castle where the great grim Peregrines sat; peering like black-masked highwaymen they marked the on-coming Pigeon. Arnaux knew them of old. Many a message was lying undelivered in that nest, many a record-bearing plume had fluttered away from its fastness. But Arnaux had faced them before, and now he came as before—on, onward, swift, but not as he had been; the deadly gun had sapped his force, had lowered his speed. On, on; and the Peregrines, biding their time, went forth like two bow-bolts; strong and lightning-swift they went against one weak and wearied.

Why tell of the race that followed? Why paint the despair of a brave little heart in sight of the home he had craved in vain? In a minute all was over. The Peregrines screeched in their triumph. Screeching and sailing, they swung to their eyrie, and the prey in their claws was the body, the last of the bright little Arnaux. There on the rocks the beaks and claws of the bandits were red with the life of the hero. Torn asunder were those matchless wings, and their records were scattered unnoticed. In sun and in storm they lay till the killers themselves were killed and their stronghold rifled. And none knew the fate of the peerless Bird till deep in the dust and rubbish

The Pirates in Ambush.

Arnaux

of that pirate-nest the avenger found, among others of its kind, a silver ring, the sacred badge of the High Homer, and read upon it the pregnant inscription:

"ARNAUX, 2590 C."

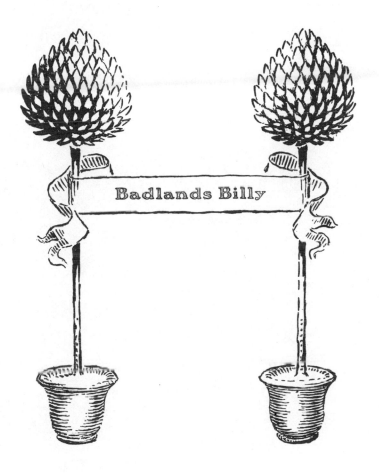

Badlands Billy

Badlands Billy
The Wolf that Won

THE HOWL BY NIGHT

O you know the three calls of the hunting Wolf: —the long-drawn deep howl, the muster, that tells of game discovered but too strong for the finder to manage alone; and the higher ululation that ringing and swelling is the cry of the pack on a hot scent; and the sharp bark coupled with a short howl that, seeming least of all, is yet a gong of doom, for this is the cry " *Close in* "—this is the finish?

We were riding the Badland Buttes, King and I, with a pack of various hunting Dogs

stringing behind or trotting alongside. The
sun had gone from the sky, and a blood-
streak marked the spot where he died, away
over Sentinel Butte. The hills were dim, the
valleys dark, when from the nearest gloom there
rolled a long-drawn cry that all men recognize
instinctively—melodious, yet with a tone in
it that sends a shudder up the spine, though
now it has lost all menace for mankind. We
listened for a moment. It was the Wolf-hunter
who broke silence: "That 's Badlands Billy;
ain't it a voice? He 's out for his beef to-night."

II

ANCIENT DAYS

In pristine days the Buffalo herds were followed by bands of Wolves that preyed on the
sick, the weak, and the wounded. When the
Buffalo were exterminated the Wolves were
hard put for support, but the Cattle came and
solved the question for them by taking the
Buffaloes' place. This caused the wolf-war.
The ranchmen offered a bounty for each Wolf

112

Badlands Billy

killed, and every cowboy out of work, was supplied with traps and poison for wolf-killing.
The very expert made this their sole business
and became known as wolvers. King Ryder
was one of these. He was a quiet, gentle-
spoken fellow, with a keen eye and an insight
into animal life that gave him especial power
over Broncos and Dogs, as well as Wolves and
Bears, though in the last two cases it was
power merely to surmise where they were and
how best to get at them. He had been a
wolver for years, and greatly surprised me by
saying that "never in all his experience had
he known a Gray-wolf to attack a human
being."

We had many camp-fire talks while the other
men were sleeping, and then it was I learned
the little that he knew about Badlands Billy.
"Six times have I seen him and the seventh
will be Sunday, you bet. He takes his long
rest then." And thus on the very ground
where it all fell out, to the noise of the night
wind and the yapping of the Coyote, interrupted
sometimes by the deep-drawn howl of the hero
himself, I heard chapters of this history which,

with others gleaned in many fields, gave me the
story of the Big Dark Wolf of Sentinel Butte

III

IN THE CAÑON

Away back in the spring of '92 a wolver was
"wolving" on the east side of the Sentinel
Mountain that so long was a principal landmark of the old Plainsmen. Pelts were not
good in May, but the bounties were high, five
dollars a head, and double for She-wolves. As
he went down to the creek one morning he
saw a Wolf coming to drink on the other side.
He had an easy shot, and on killing it found
it was a nursing She-wolf. Evidently her family were somewhere near, so he spent two or
three days searching in all the likely places, but
found no clue to the den.

Two weeks afterward, as the wolver rode
down an adjoining cañon, he saw a Wolf come
out of a hole. The ever-ready rifle flew up,
and another ten-dollar scalp was added to his
string. Now he dug into the den and found

Badlands Billy

the litter, a most surprising one indeed, for it consisted not of the usual five or six Wolf-pups, but of eleven, and these, strange to say, were of two sizes, five of them larger and older than the other six. Here were two distinct families with one mother, and as he added their scalps to his string of trophies the truth dawned on the hunter. One lot was surely the family of the She-wolf he had killed two weeks before. The case was clear: the little ones awaiting the mother that was never to come, had whined piteously and more loudly as their hunger-pangs increased; the other mother passing had heard the Cubs; her heart was tender now, her own little ones had so recently come, and she cared for the orphans, carried them to her own den, and was providing for the double family when the rifleman had cut the gentle chapter short.

Many a wolver has dug into a wolf-den to find nothing. The old Wolves or possibly the Cubs themselves often dig little side pockets and off galleries, and when an enemy is breaking in they hide in these. The loose earth conceals the small pocket and thus the Cubs escape. When the wolver retired with his scalps he did not know that the biggest of all the Cubs, was still in the den, and even had he waited about for two hours, he might have been no wiser. Three hours later the sun went down and there was a slight scratching afar in the hole; first two little gray paws, then a small black nose appeared in a soft sand-pile to one side of the den. At length the Cub came forth from his hiding. He had been frightened by the attack on the den; now he was perplexed by its condition.

It was thrice as large as it had been and open at the top now. Lying near were things that smelled like his brothers and sisters, but they were repellent to him. He was filled with fear as he sniffed at them, and sneaked aside into a thicket of grass, as a Night-hawk boomed over his head. He crouched all night in that thicket. He did not dare to go near the den, and knew not where else he could go. The next morning when two Vultures came swooping down on the bodies, the Wolf-cub ran off in the thicket, and seeking its deepest cover, was led down a ravine to a wide valley. Sud-

116

denly there arose from the grass a big She-
wolf, like his mother, yet different, a stranger,
and instinctively the stray Cub sank to the
earth, as the old Wolf bounded on him. No
doubt the Cub had been taken for some law-
ful prey, but a whiff set that right. She stood
over him for an instant. He grovelled at her
feet. The impulse to kill him or at least give
him a shake died away. He had the smell of
a young Cub. Her own were about his age,
her heart was touched, and when he found
courage enough to put his nose up and smell
her nose, she made no angry demonstration
except a short half-hearted growl. Now,
however, he had smelled something that he
sorely needed. He had not fed since the
day before, and when the old Wolf turned to
leave him, he tumbled after her on clumsy
puppy legs. Had the Mother-wolf been far
from home he must soon have been left behind, but the nearest hollow was the chosen
place, and the Cub arrived at the den's mouth
soon after the Mother-wolf.

A stranger is an enemy, and the old one
rushing forth to the defense, met the Cub again,

and again was restrained by something that rose in her responsive to the smell. The Cub had thrown himself on his back in utter submission, but that did not prevent his nose reporting to him the good thing almost within reach. The She-wolf went into the den and curled herself about her brood; the Cub persisted in following. She snarled as he approached her own little ones, but disarming wrath each time by submission and his very cubhood, he was presently among her brood, helping himself to what he wanted so greatly, and thus he adopted himself into her family. In a few days he was so much one of them that the mother forgot about his being a stranger. Yet he was different from them in several ways—older by two weeks, stronger, and marked on the neck and shoulders with what afterward grew to be a dark mane.

Little Duskymane could not have been happier in his choice of a foster-mother, for the Yellow Wolf was not only a good hunter with a fund of cunning, but she was a Wolf of modern ideas as well. The old tricks of tolling a Prairie Dog, relaying for Antelope, houghing a

Billy finds a Foster-mother.

Badlands Billy

Bronco or flanking a Steer she had learned
partly from instinct and partly from the example of her more experienced relatives, when
they joined to form the winter bands. But,
just as necessary nowadays, she had learned
that all men carry guns, that guns are irresistible, that the only way to avoid them is by keeping out of sight while the sun is up, and yet
that at night they are harmless. She had a
fair comprehension of traps, indeed she had
been in one once, and though she left a toe
behind in pulling free, it was a toe most advan-
tageously disposed of; thenceforth, though not
comprehending the nature of the trap, she was
thoroughly imbued with the horror of it, with
the idea indeed that iron is dangerous, and at
any price it should be avoided.

On one occasion, when she and five others
were planning to raid a Sheep yard, she held
back at the last minute because some new-
strung wires appeared. The others rushed in
to find the Sheep beyond their reach, themselves in a death-trap.

Thus she had learned the newer dangers,
and while it is unlikely that she had any clear

mental conception of them she had acquired a wholesome distrust of all things strange, and a horror of one or two in particular that proved her lasting safeguard. Each year she raised her brood successfully and the number of Yellow Wolves increased in the country. Guns, traps, men and the new animals they brought had been learned, but there was yet another lesson before her—a terrible one indeed.

About the time Duskymane's brothers were a month old his foster-mother returned in a strange condition. She was frothing at the mouth, her legs trembled, and she fell in a convulsion near the doorway of the den, but recovering, she came in. Her jaws quivered, her teeth rattled a little as she tried to lick the little ones; she seized her own front leg and bit it so as not to bite them, but at length she grew quieter and calmer. The Cubs had retreated in fear to a far pocket, but now they returned and crowded about her to seek their usual food. The mother recovered, but was very ill for two or three days, and those days with the poison in her system worked disaster for the brood. They were terribly sick; only

Badlands Billy

the strongest could survive, and when the trial
of strength was over, the den contained only
the old one and the Black-maned Cub, the
one she had adopted.   Thus little Duskymane
became her sole charge; all her strength was
devoted to feeding him, and he thrived apace.

Wolves are quick to learn certain things.
The reactions of smell are the greatest that a
Wolf can feel, and thenceforth both Cub and
foster-mother experienced a quick, unreasoning
sense of fear and hate the moment the smell of
strychnine reached them.

IV

THE RUDIMENTS OF WOLF TRAINING

With the sustenance of seven at his service
the little Wolf had every reason to grow, and
when in the autumn he began to follow his
mother on her hunting trips he was as tall as
she was.   Now a change of region was forced
on them, for numbers of little Wolves were
growing up.   Sentinel Butte, the rocky fastness
of the plains, was claimed by many that were

123

big and strong; the weaker must move out, and with them Yellow Wolf and the Dusky Cub.

Wolves have no language in the sense that man has; their vocabulary is probably limited to a dozen howls, barks, and grunts expressing the simplest emotions; but they have several other modes of conveying ideas, and one very special method of spreading information—the Wolf-telephone. Scattered over their range are a number of recognized "centrals." Sometimes these are stones, sometimes the angle of cross-trails, sometimes a Buffalo-skull—indeed, any conspicuous object near a main trail is used. A Wolf calling here, as a Dog does at a telegraph post, or a Muskrat at a certain mud-pie point, leaves his body-scent and learns what other visitors have been there recently to do the same. He learns also whence they came and where they went, as well as something about their condition, whether hunted, hungry, gorged, or sick. By this system of registration a Wolf knows where his friends, as well as his foes, are to be found. And Duskymane, following after the Yellow Wolf, was taught the places and uses of the many

Badlands Billy

signal-stations without any conscious attempt at teaching on the part of his foster-mother. Example backed by his native instincts was indeed the chief teacher, but on one occasion at least there was something very like the effort of a human parent to guard her child in danger.

The Dark Cub had learned the rudiments of Wolf life: that the way to fight Dogs is to run, and to fight as you run, never grapple, but snap, snap, snap, and make for the rough country where Horses cannot bring their riders.

He learned not to bother about the Coyotes that follow for the pickings when you hunt; you cannot catch them and they do you no harm.

He knew he must not waste time dashing after Birds that alight on the ground; and that he must keep away from the little black and white Animal with the bushy tail. It is not very good to eat, and it is very, very bad to smell.

Poison! Oh, he never forgot that smell from the day when the den was cleared of all his foster-brothers.

Badlands Billy

He now knew that the first move in attacking Sheep was to scatter them; a lone Sheep is a foolish and easy prey; that the way to round up a band of Cattle was to frighten a Calf.

He learned that he must always attack a Steer behind, a Sheep in front, and a Horse in the middle, that is, on the flank, and never, never attack a man at all, never even face him. But an important lesson was added to these, one in which the mother consciously taught him of a secret foe.

V

THE LESSON ON TRAPS

A Calf had died in branding-time and now, two weeks later, was in its best state for perfect taste, not too fresh, not over-ripe—that is, in a Wolf's opinion—and the wind carried this information afar. The Yellow Wolf and Duskymane were out for supper, though not yet knowing where, when the tidings of veal arrived, and they trotted up the wind. The Calf was in an open place, and plain to be seen in the moonlight. A Dog would have trotted

Badlands Billy

right up to the carcass, an old-time Wolf might have done so, but constant war had developed constant vigilance in the Yellow Wolf, and trusting nothing and no one but her nose, she slacked her speed to a walk. On coming in easy view she stopped, and for long swung her nose, submitting the wind to the closest possible chemical analysis. She tried it with her finest tests, blew all the membranes clean again and tried it once more; and this was the report of the trusty nostrils, yes, the unanimous report. First, rich and racy smell of Calf, seventy per cent.; smells of grass, bugs, wood, flowers, trees, sand, and other uninteresting negations, fifteen per cent.; smell of her Cub and herself, positive but ignorable, ten per cent.; smell of human tracks, two per cent.; smell of smoke, one per cent.; of sweaty leather smell, one per cent.; of human body-scent (not discernible in some samples), one-half per cent.; smell of iron, a trace.

The old Wolf crouched a little but sniffed hard with swinging nose; the young Wolf imitatively did the same. She backed off to a greater distance; the Cub stood. She gave a

127

p. c.	
=	70
}	15
=	10
=	2
=	1
=	·1
=	½
=	a trace
	100

low whine; he followed unwillingly. She circled around the tempting carcass; a new smell was recorded—Coyote trail-scent, soon followed by Coyote body-scent. Yes, there they were sneaking along a near ridge, and now as she passed to one side the samples changed, the wind had lost nearly every trace of Calf; miscellaneous, commonplace, and uninteresting smells were there instead. The human track-scent was as before, the trace of leather was gone, but fully one-half per cent. of iron-odor, and body-smell of man raised to nearly two per cent.

Fully alarmed, she conveyed her fear to the Cub, by her rigid pose, her air intent, and her slightly bristling mane.

She continued her round. At one time on a high place the human body-scent was doubly strong, then as she dropped it faded. Then the wind brought the full calf-odor with several track-scents of Coyotes and sundry Birds. Her suspicions were lulling as in a smalling circle she neared the tempting feast from the windward side. She had even advanced straight toward it for a few steps when the sweaty

Badlands Billy

leather sang loud and strong again, and smoke and iron mingled like two strands of a particolored yarn. Centring all her attention on this, she advanced within two leaps of the Calf. There on the ground was a scrap of leather, telling also of a human touch, close at hand the Calf, and now the iron and smoke on the full vast smell of Calf were like a snake trail across the trail of a whole Beef herd. It was so slight that the Cub, with the appetite and impatience of youth, pressed up against his mother's shoulder to go past and eat without delay. She seized him by the neck and flung him back. A stone struck by his feet rolled forward and stopped with a peculiar clink. The danger smell was greatly increased at this, and the Yellow Wolf backed slowly from the feast, the Cub unwillingly following.

As he looked wistfully he saw the Coyotes drawing nearer, mindful chiefly to avoid the Wolves. He watched their really cautious advance; it seemed like heedless rushing compared with his mother's approach. The Calf smell rolled forth in exquisite and overpowering excellence now, for they were tearing the

meat, when a sharp clank was heard and a yelp from a Coyote. At the same time the quiet night was shocked with a roar and a flash of fire. Heavy shots spattered Calf and Coyotes, and yelping like beaten Dogs they scattered, excepting one that was killed and a second struggling in the trap set here by the ever-active wolvers. The air was charged with the hateful smells redoubled now, and horrid smells additional. The Yellow Wolf glided down a hollow and led her Cub away in flight, but, as they went, they saw a man rush from the bank near where the mother's nose had warned her of the human scent. They saw him kill the caught Coyote and set the traps for more.

VI

THE BEGUILING OF THE YELLOW WOLF

The life game is a hard game, for we may win ten thousand times, and if we fail but once our gain is gone. How many hundred times had the Yellow Wolf scorned the traps; how many Cubs she had trained to do the same!

Their narrow Escape from Trap and Gun.

Badlands Billy

Of all the dangers to her life she best knew traps.

October had come; the Cub was now much taller than the mother. The wolver had seen them once—a Yellow Wolf followed by another, whose long, awkward legs, big, soft feet, thin neck, and skimpy tail proclaimed him this year's Cub. The record of the dust and sand said that the old one had lost a right front toe, and that the young one was of giant size.

It was the wolver that thought to turn the carcass of the Calf to profit, but he was disappointed in getting Coyotes instead of Wolves. It was the beginning of the trapping season, for this month fur is prime. A young trapper often fastens the bait on the trap; an experienced one does not. A good trapper will even put the bait at one place and the trap ten or twenty feet away, but at a spot that the Wolf is likely to cross in circling. A favorite plan is to hide three or four traps around an open place, and scatter some scraps of meat in the middle. The traps are buried out of sight after being smoked to hide the taint of hands and iron. Sometimes no bait is used except a little piece of cotton or a tuft of feathers that may catch the Wolf's eye or pique its curiosity and tempt it to circle on the fateful, treacherous ground. A good trapper varies his methods continually so that the Wolves cannot learn his ways. Their only safeguards are perpetual vigilance and distrust of all smells that are known to be of man.

The wolver, with a load of the strongest steel traps, had begun his autumn work on the ' Cottonwood.'

An old Buffalo trail crossing the river followed a little draw that climbed the hills to the level upland. All animals use these trails, Wolves and Foxes as well as Cattle and Deer: they are the main thoroughfares. A cottonwood stump not far from where it plunged to the gravelly stream was marked with Wolf signs that told the wolver of its use. Here was an excellent place for traps, not on the trail, for Cattle were here in numbers, but twenty yards away on a level, sandy spot he set four traps in a twelve-foot square. Near each he scattered two or three scraps of meat; three or four white feathers on a spear of grass

134

Badlands Billy

in the middle completed the setting. No human eye, few animal noses, could have detected the hidden danger of that sandy ground, when the sun and wind and the sand itself had dissipated the man-track taint.

The Yellow Wolf had seen and passed, and taught her giant son to pass, such traps a thousand times before.

The Cattle came to water in the heat of the day. They strung down the Buffalo path as once the Buffalo did. The little Vesper-birds flitted before them, the Cowbirds rode on them, and the Prairie-dogs chattered at them, just as they once did at the Buffalo.

Down from the gray-green mesa with its green-gray rocks, they marched with imposing solemnity, importance, and directness of purpose. Some frolicsome Calves, playing alongside the trail, grew sober and walked behind their mothers as the river flat was reached. The old Cow that headed the procession sniffed suspiciously as she passed the "trap set," but it was far away, otherwise she would have pawed and bellowed over the scraps of bloody beef till every trap was sprung and harmless.

Badlands Billy

But she led to the river.   After all had drunk their fill they lay down on the nearest bank till late afternoon.   Then their unheard dinner-gong aroused them, and started them on the backward march to where the richest pastures grew.

One or two small birds had picked at the scraps of meat, some blue-bottle flies buzzed about, but the sinking sun saw the sandy mask untouched.

A brown Marsh Hawk came skimming over the river flat as the sun began his color play. Blackbirds dashed into thickets, and easily avoided his clumsy pounce.   It was too early for the Mice, but, as he skimmed the ground, his keen eye caught the flutter of feathers by the trap and turned his flight.   The feathers in their uninteresting emptiness were exposed before he was near, but now he saw the scraps of meat.   Guileless of cunning, he alighted and was devouring a second lump when— *clank*—the dust was flirted high and the Marsh Hawk was held by his toes, struggling vainly in the jaws of a powerful wolf-trap. He was not much hurt.   His ample wings win-

Badlands Billy

nowed from time to time, in efforts to be free,
but he was helpless, even as a Sparrow might
be in a rat-trap, and when the sun had played
his fierce chromatic scale, his swan-song sung,
and died as he dies only in the blazing west,
and the shades had fallen on the melodramatic
scene of the Mouse in the elephant-trap, there
was a deep, rich sound on the high flat butte,
answered by another, neither very long, neither
repeated, and both instinctive rather than necessary.   One was the muster-call of an ordinary
Wolf, the other the answer of a very big male,
not a pair in this case, but mother and son—
Yellow Wolf and Duskymane. They came trotting together down the Buffalo trail.   They
paused at the telephone box on the hill and
again at the old cottonwood root, and were
making for the river when the Hawk in the
trap fluttered his wings.   The old Wolf turned
toward him,—a wounded bird on the ground
surely, and she rushed forward.   Sun and sand
soon burn all trail-scents; there was nothing to
warn her.   She sprang on the flopping bird
and a chop of her jaws ended his troubles, but
a horrid sound—the gritting of her teeth on

137

steel—told her of peril. She dropped the Hawk and sprang backward from the dangerous ground, but landed in the second trap. High on her foot its death-grip closed, and leaping with all her strength, to escape, she set her fore foot in another of the lurking grips of steel. Never had a trap been so baited before. Never was she so unsuspicious. Never was catch more sure. Fear and fury filled the old Wolf's heart; she tugged and strained, she chewed the chains, she snarled and foamed. One trap with its buried log, she might have dragged; with two, she was helpless. Struggle as she might, it only worked those relentless jaws more deeply into her feet. She snapped wildly at the air; she tore the dead Hawk into shreds; she roared the short, barking roar of a crazy Wolf. She bit at the traps, at her cub, at herself. She tore her legs that were held; she gnawed in frenzy at her flank, she chopped off her tail in her madness; she splintered all her teeth on the steel, and filled her bleeding, foaming jaws with clay and sand.

She struggled till she fell, and writhed about

THE DESPAIR OF THE YELLOW-WOLF

or lay like dead, till strong enough to rise and
grind the chains again with her teeth.

And so the night passed by.

And Duskymane? Where was he? The
feeling of the time when his foster-mother had
come home poisoned, now returned; but he was
even more afraid of her. She seemed filled
with fighting hate. He held away and whined
a little; he slunk off and came back when she
lay still, only to retreat again, as she sprang
forward, raging at him, and then renewed her
efforts at the traps. He did not understand it,
but he knew this much, she was in terrible
trouble, and the cause seemed to be the same
as that which had scared them the night they
had ventured near the Calf.

Duskymane hung about all night, fearing to
go near, not knowing what to do, and helpless
as his mother.

At dawn the next day a sheepherder seeking
lost Sheep discovered her from a neighboring
hill. A signal mirror called the wolver from
his camp. Duskymane saw the new danger.
He was a mere Cub, though so tall; he could
not face the man, and fled at his approach.

The wolver rode up to the sorry, tattered, bleeding She-wolf in the trap. He raised his rifle and soon the struggling stopped.

The wolver read the trail and the signs about, and remembering those he had read before, he divined that this was the Wolf with the great Cub—the She-wolf of Sentinel Butte.

Duskymane heard the "crack" as he scurried off into cover. He could scarcely know what it meant, but he never saw his kind old foster-mother again. Thenceforth he must face the world alone.

VII

THE YOUNG WOLF WINS A PLACE AND FAME

Instinct is no doubt a Wolf's first and best guide, but gifted parents are a great start in life. The dusky-maned cub had had a mother of rare excellence and he reaped the advantage of all her cleverness. He had inherited an exquisite nose and had absolute confidence in its admonitions. Mankind has difficulty in recognizing the power of nostrils. A Gray-wolf can glance over the morning wind as a man does

Badlands Billy

over his newspaper, and get all the latest news. He can swing over the ground and have the minutest information of every living creature that has walked there within many hours. His nose even tells which way it ran, and in a word renders a statement of every animal that recently crossed his trail, whence it came, and whither it went.

That power had Duskymane in the highest degree; his broad, moist nose was evidence of it to all who are judges of such things. Added to this, his frame was of unusual power and endurance, and last, he had early learned a deep distrust of everything strange, and, call it what we will, shyness, wariness or suspicion, it was worth more to him than all his cleverness. It was this as much as his physical powers that made a success of his life. Might is right in wolf-land, and Duskymane and his mother had been driven out of Sentinel Butte. But it was a very delectable land and he kept drifting back to his native mountain. One or two big Wolves there resented his coming. They drove him off several times, yet each time he returned he was

better able to face them; and before he was
eighteen months old he had defeated all rivals
and established himself again on his native
ground; where he lived like a robber baron,
levying tribute on the rich lands about him and
finding safety in the rocky fastness.

Wolver Ryder often hunted in that country,
and before long, he came across a five-and-one-
half-inch track, the foot-print of a giant Wolf.
Roughly reckoned, twenty to twenty-five
pounds of weight or six inches of stature is a fair
allowance for each inch of a Wolf's foot; this
Wolf therefore stood thirty-three inches at the
shoulder and weighed about one hundred and
forty pounds, by far the largest Wolf he had ever
met. King had lived in Goat country, and now
in Goat language he exclaimed: "You bet,
ain't that an old Billy?" Thus by trivial
chance it was that Duskymane was known to
his foe, as 'Badlands Billy.'

Ryder was familiar with the muster-call of
the Wolves, the long, smooth cry, but Billy's
had a singular feature, a slurring that was always distinctive. Ryder had heard this before,
in the Cottonwood Cañon, and when at length

O - w - w - w

Badlands Billy

he got a sight of the big Wolf with the black mane, it struck him that this was also the Cub of the old Yellow fury that he had trapped.

These were among the things he told me as we sat by the fire at night. I knew of the early days when any one could trap or poison Wolves, of the passing of those days, with the passing of the simple Wolves; of the new race of Wolves with new cunning that were defying the methods of the ranchmen, and increasing steadily in numbers. Now the wolver told me of the various ventures that Penroof had made with different kinds of Hounds: of Foxhounds too thin-skinned to fight; of Greyhounds that were useless when the animal was out of sight; of Danes too heavy for the rough country, and, last, of the composite pack with some of all kinds, including at times a Bull-terrier to lead them in the final fight.

He told of hunts after Coyotes, which usually were successful because the Coyotes sought the plains, and were easily caught by the Grey-hounds. He told of killing some small Gray-wolves with this very pack, usually at the cost of the one that led them; but above all he dwelt on the wonderful prowess of "that thar cussed old Black Wolf of Sentinel Butte," and related the many attempts to run him down or corner him—an unbroken array of failures. For the big Wolf, with exasperating persistence, continued to live on the finest stock of the Penroof brand, and each year was teaching more Wolves how to do the same with perfect impunity.

I listened even as gold-hunters listen to stories of treasure trove, for these were the things of my world. These things indeed were uppermost in all our minds, for the Penroof pack was lying around our camp-fire now. We were out after Badlands Billy.

VIII

THE VOICE IN THE NIGHT AND THE BIG TRACK IN THE MORNING

One night late in September after the last streak of light was gone from the west and the Coyotes had begun their yapping chorus, a deep, booming sound was heard. King took out his pipe, turned his head and said: "That's

" ' That 's him.' "

Badlands Billy

him—that 's old Billy. He 's been watching us all day from some high place, and now when the guns are useless he 's here to have a little fun with us."

Two or three Dogs arose, with bristling manes, for they clearly recognized that this was no Coyote. They rushed out into the night, but did not go far; their brawling sounds were suddenly varied by loud yelps, and they came running back to the shelter of the fire. One was so badly cut in the shoulder that he was useless for the rest of the hunt. Another was hurt in the flank—it seemed the less serious wound, and yet next morning the hunters buried that second Dog.

The men were furious. They vowed speedy vengeance, and at dawn were off on the trail. The Coyotes yelped their dawning song, but they melted into the hills when the light was strong. The hunters searched about for the big Wolf's track, hoping that the Hounds would be able to take it up and find him, but they either could not or would not.

They found a Coyote, however, and within a few hundred yards they killed him. It was a victory, I suppose, for Coyotes kill Calves and Sheep, but somehow I felt the common thought of all: "Mighty brave Dogs for a little Coyote, but they could not face the big Wolf last night."

Young Penroof, as though in answer to one of the unput questions, said:

"Say, boys, I believe old Billy had a hull bunch of Wolves with him last night."

"Did n't see but one track," said King gruffly.

In this way the whole of October slipped by; all day hard riding after doubtful trails, following the Dogs, who either could not keep the big trail or feared to do so, and again and again we had news of damage done by the Wolf; sometimes a cowboy would report it to us; and sometimes we found the carcasses ourselves. A few of these we poisoned, though it is considered a very dangerous thing to do while running Dogs. The end of the month found us a weather-beaten, dispirited lot of men, with a worn-out lot of Horses, and a footsore pack, reduced in numbers from ten to seven. So far we had killed only one Gray-

Badlands Billy

wolf and three Coyotes; Badlands Billy had killed at least a dozen Cows and Dogs at fifty dollars a head. Some of the boys decided to give it up and go home, so King took advantage of their going, to send a letter, asking for reën-forcements including all the spare Dogs at the ranch.

During the two days' wait we rested our Horses, shot some game, and prepared for a harder hunt. Late on the second day the new Dogs arrived—eight beauties—and raised the working pack to fifteen.

The weather now turned much cooler, and in the morning, to the joy of the wolvers, the ground was white with snow. This surely meant success. With cool weather for the Dogs and Horses to run; with the big Wolf not far away, for he had been heard the night before; and with tracking snow, so that once found he could not baffle us,—escape for him was im-possible.

We were up at dawn, but before we could get away, three men came riding into camp. They were the Penroof boys back again. The change of weather had changed their minds;

they knew that with snow we might have luck.

 "Remember now," said King, as all were mounting, "we don't want any but Badlands Billy this trip. Get him an' we kin bust up the hull combination. It is a five-and-a-half-inch track."

And each measured off on his quirt handle, or on his glove, the exact five and a half inches that was to be used in testing the tracks he might find.

Not more than an hour elapsed before we got a signal from the rider who had gone westward. One shot: that means "attention," a pause while counting ten, then two shots: that means "*come on.*"

King gathered the Dogs and rode direct to the distant figure on the hill. All hearts beat high with hope, and we were not disappointed. Some small Wolf tracks had been found, but here at last was the big track, nearly six inches long. Young Penroof wanted to yell and set out at full gallop. It was like hunting a Lion; it was like finding happiness long deferred. The hunter knows nothing more inspiring than

the clean-cut line of fresh tracks that is leading
to a wonderful animal, he has long been hunting in vain. How King's eye gleamed as he
gloated over the sign!

IX

RUN DOWN AT LAST

It was the roughest of all rough riding. It
was a far longer hunt than we had expected, and
was full of little incidents, for that endless line
of marks was a minute history of all that the
big Wolf had done the night before. Here he
had circled at the telephone box and looked for
news; there he had paused to examine an old
skull; here he had shied off and swung cautiously up wind to examine something that
proved to be an old tin can; there at length he
had mounted a low hill and sat down, probably
giving the muster-howl, for two Wolves had
come to him from different directions, and they
then had descended to the river flat where the
Cattle would seek shelter during the storm.
Here all three had visited a Buffalo skull;

151

there they trotted in line; and yonder they separated, going three different ways, to meet—yes
—here—oh, what a sight, a fine Cow ripped
open, left dead and *uneaten*. Not to their taste,
it seems, for see! within a mile is another killed
by them. Not six hours ago, they had feasted.
Here their trails scatter again, but not far, and
the snow tells plainly how each had lain down
to sleep. The Hounds' manes bristled as they
sniffed those places. King had held the Dogs
well in hand, but now they were greatly excited.
We came to a hill whereon the Wolves had
turned and faced our way, then fled at full
speed,—so said the trail,—and now it was clear
that they had watched us from that hill, and
were not far away.

The pack kept well together, because the
Greyhounds, seeing no quarry, were merely
puttering about among the other Dogs, or running back with the Horses. We went as fast
as we could, for the Wolves were speeding. Up
mesas and down coulees we rode, sticking
closely to the Dogs, though it was the roughest
country that could be picked. One gully after
another, an hour and another hour, and still the

Badlands Billy

threefold track went bounding on; another
hour and no change, but interminable climbing,
sliding, struggling, through brush and over
boulders, guided by the far-away yelping of the
Dogs.

Now the chase led downward to the low
valley of the river, where there was scarcely any
snow. Jumping and scrambling down hills,
recklessly leaping dangerous gullies and slip-
pery rocks, we felt that we could not hold out
much longer; when on the lowest, dryest level
the pack split, some went up, some went down,
and others straight on. Oh, how King did
swear! He knew at once what it meant. The
Wolves had scattered, and so had divided the
pack. Three Dogs after a Wolf would have
no chance, four could not kill him, two would
certainly be killed. And yet this was the first
encouraging sign we had seen, for it meant that
the Wolves were hard pressed. We spurred
ahead to stop the Dogs, to pick for them the
only trail. But that was not so easy. Without
snow here and with countless Dog tracks, we
were foiled. All we could do was to let the
Dogs choose, but keep them to a single choice.

Badlands Billy

Away we went as before, hoping, yet fearing that we were not on the right track. The Dogs ran well, very fast indeed. This was a bad sign, King said, but we could not get sight of the track because the Dogs overran it before we came.

After a two-mile run the chase led upward again in snow country; the Wolf was sighted, but to our disgust, we were on the track of the smallest one.

"I thought so," growled young Penroof. "Dogs was altogether too keen for a serious proposition. Kind o' surprised it ain't turned out a Jack-rabbit."

Within another mile he had turned to bay in a willow thicket. We heard him howl the long-drawn howl for help, and before we could reach the place King saw the Dogs recoil and scatter. A minute later there sped from the far side of the thicket a small Gray-wolf and a Black One of very much greater size.

"By golly, if he did n't yell for help, and Billy come back to help him; that 's great!" exclaimed the wolver. And my heart went out to the brave old Wolf that refused to escape by abandoning his friend.

154

Badlands Billy

The next hour was a hard repetition of the gully riding, but it was on the highlands where there was snow, and when again the pack was split, we strained every power and succeeded in keeping them on the big " five-fifty track," that already was wearing for me the glamour of romance.

Evidently the Dogs preferred either of the others, but we got them going at last. Another half hour's hard work and far ahead, as I rose to a broad flat plain, I had my first glimpse of the Big Black Wolf of Sentinel Butte.

" Hurrah! Badlands Billy! Hurrah! Badlands Billy!" I shouted in salute, and the others took up the cry.

We were on his track at last, thanks to himself. The Dogs joined in with a louder baying, the Greyhounds yelped and made straight for him, and the Horses sniffed and sprang more gamely as they caught the thrill. The only silent one was the black-maned Wolf, and as I marked his size and power, and above all his long and massive jaws, I knew why the Dogs preferred some other trail.

With head and tail low he was bounding over

155

the snow. His tongue was lolling long; plainly he was hard pressed. The wolvers' hands flew to their revolvers, though he was three hundred yards ahead; they were out for blood, not sport. But an instant later he had sunk from view in the nearest sheltered cañon.

Now which way would he go, up or down the cañon? Up was toward his mountain, down was better cover. King and I thought "up," so pressed westward along the ridge. But the others rode eastward, watching for a chance to shoot.

Soon we had ridden out of hearing. We were wrong—the Wolf had gone down, but we heard no shooting. The cañon was crossable here; we reached the other side and then turned back at a gallop, scanning the snow for a trail, the hills for a moving form, or the wind for a sound of life.

"Squeak, squeak," went our saddle leathers, "puff—puff" our Horses, and their feet "ka-ka-lump, ka-ka-lump."

Badlands Billy

X

We were back opposite to where the Wolf had plunged, but saw no sign. We rode at an easy gallop, on eastward, a mile, and still on, when King gasped out, "Look at that!" A dark spot was moving on the snow ahead. We put on speed. Another dark spot appeared, and another, but they were not going fast. In five minutes we were near them, to find—three of our own Greyhounds. They had lost sight of the game, and with that their interest waned. Now they were seeking us. We saw nothing there of the chase or of the other hunters. But hastening to the next ridge we stumbled on the trail we sought and followed as hard as though in view. Another cañon came in our path, and as we rode and looked for a place to cross, a wild din of Hounds came from its brushy depth. The clamor grew and passed up the middle.

We raced along the rim, hoping to see the game. The Dogs appeared near the farther side, not in a pack, but a long, straggling line.

157

Badlands Billy

In five minutes more they rose to the edge, and ahead of them was the great Black Wolf. He was loping as before, head and tail low. Power was plain in every limb, and double power in his jaws and neck, but I thought his bounds were shorter now, and that they had lost their spring. The Dogs slowly reached the upper level, and sighting him they broke into a feeble cry; they, too, were nearly spent. The Greyhounds saw the chase, and leaving us they scrambled down the cañon and up the other side at impetuous speed that would surely break them down, while we rode, vainly seeking means of crossing.

How the wolver raved to see the pack lead off in the climax of the chase, and himself held up behind. But he rode and wrathed and still rode, up to where the cañon dwindled—rough land and a hard ride. As we neared the great flat mountain, the feeble cry of the pack was heard again from the south, then toward the high Butte's side, and just a trifle louder now. We reined in on a hillock and scanned the snow. A moving speck appeared, then others, not bunched, but in a straggling train, and at

Badlands Billy

times there was a far faint cry. They were
headed toward us, coming on, yes! coming, but
so slowly, for not one was really running now.
There was the grim old Cow-killer limping over
the ground, and far behind a Greyhound, and
another, and farther still, the other Dogs in
order of their speed, slowly, gamely, dragging
themselves on that pursuit. Many hours of
hardest toil had done their work. The Wolf had
vainly sought to fling them off. Now was his
hour of doom, for he was spent; they still had
some reserve. Straight to us for a time they
came, skirting the base of the mountain, crawling.

We could not cross to join them, so held our
breath and gazed with ravenous eyes. They
were nearer now, the wind brought feeble notes
from the Hounds. The big Wolf turned to the
steep ascent, up a well-known trail, it seemed,
for he made no slip. My heart went with him,
for he had come back to rescue his friend, and
a momentary thrill of pity came over us both,
as we saw him glance around and drag himself
up the sloping way, to die on his mountain.
There was no escape for him, beset by fifteen

Dogs with men to back them. He was not walking, but tottering upward; the Dogs behind in line, were now doing a little better, were nearing him. We could hear them gasping; we scarcely heard them bay—they had no breath for that; upward the grim procession went, circling a spur of the Butte and along a ledge that climbed and narrowed, then dropped for a few yards to a shelf that reared above the cañon. The foremost Dogs were closing, fearless of a foe so nearly spent.

Here in the narrowest place, where one wrong step meant death, the great Wolf turned and faced them. With fore-feet braced, with head low and tail a little raised, his dusky mane a-bristling, his glittering tusks laid bare, but uttering no sound that we could hear, he faced the crew. His legs were weak with toil, but his neck, his jaws, and his heart were strong, and—now all you who love the Dogs had better close the book—on—up and down—fifteen to one, they came, the swiftest first, and how it was done, the eye could scarcely see, but even as a stream of water pours on a rock to be splashed in broken jets aside, that stream of

" The Great Wolf turned and faced Them."

Badlands Billy

Dogs came pouring down the path, in single file perforce, and Duskymane received them as they came. A feeble spring, a counter-lunge, a gash, and " Fango 's down," has lost his foothold and is gone. Dander and Coalie close and try to clinch; a rush, a heave, and they are fallen from that narrow path. Blue-spot then, backed by mighty Oscar and fearless Tige—but the Wolf is next the rock and the flash of combat clears to show him there alone, the big Dogs gone; the rest close in, the hindmost force the foremost on—down—to their death. Slash, chop and heave, from the swiftest to the biggest, to the last, down—down— he sent them whirling from the ledge to the gaping gulch below, where rocks and snags of trunks were sharp to do their work.

In fifty seconds it was done. The rock had splashed the stream aside—the Penroof pack was all wiped out; and Badlands Billy stood there, alone again on his mountain.

A moment he waited to look for more to come. There were no more, the pack was dead; but waiting he got his breath, then raising his voice for the first time in that fatal scene, he feebly gave a long yell of triumph, and scaling the next low bank, was screened from view in a cañon of Sentinel Butte.

We stared like men of stone. The guns in our hands were forgotten. It was all so quick, so final. We made no move till the Wolf was gone. It was not far to the place: we went on foot to see if any had escaped. Not one was left alive. We could do nothing—we could say nothing.

O - w - w - w

XI

THE HOWL AT SUNSET

A week later we were riding the upper trail back of the Chimney Pot, King and I. "The old man is pretty sick of it," he said. "He'd sell out if he could. He don't know what's the next move."

The sun went down beyond Sentinel Butte. It was dusk as we reached the turn that led to Dumont's place, and a deep-toned rolling howl came from the river flat below, followed by a number of higher-pitched howls in answering chorus. We could see nothing, but we lis-

164

Badlands Billy

tened hard. The song was repeated, the hunt-
ing-cry of the Wolves. It faded, the night was
stirred by another, the sharp bark and the short
howl, the signal " close in " ; a bellow came up,
very short, for it was cut short.

And King as he touched his Horse said
grimly: " That 's him, he is out with the pack,
an' thar goes another Beef."

The Boy and the Lynx

The Boy and the Lynx

THE BOY

E was barely fifteen, a lover of sport and uncommonly keen, even for a beginner. Flocks of Wild Pigeons had been coming all day across the blue Lake of Caygeonull, and perching in lines on the dead limbs of the great rampikes that stood as monuments of fire, around the little clearing in the forest, they afforded tempting marks; but he followed them for hours in vain. They seemed to know the exact range of the old-fashioned shotgun and rose on noisy wings each time before he was near

enough to fire. At length a small flock scattered among the low green trees that grew about the spring, near the log shanty, and taking advantage of the cover, Thorburn went in gently. He caught sight of a single Pigeon close to him, took a long aim and fired. A sharp crack resounded at almost the same time and the bird fell dead. Thorburn rushed to seize the prize just as a tall young man stepped into view and picked it up.

"Hello, Corney! you got my bird!"

"Your burrud! Sure yours flew away thayre. I saw them settle hayer and thought I'd make sure of wan with the rifle."

A careful examination showed that a rifle-ball as well as a charge of shot had struck the Pigeon. The gunners had fired on the same bird. Both enjoyed the joke, though it had its serious side, for food as well as ammunition was scarce in that backwoods home.

Corney, a superb specimen of a six-foot Irish-Canadian in early manhood, now led away to the log shanty where the very scarcity of luxuries and the roughness of their lives were sources of merriment. For the Colts, though

The Boy and the Lynx

born and bred in the backwoods of Canada, had lost nothing of the spirit that makes the Irish blood a world-wide synonym of heartiness and wit.

Corney was the eldest son of a large family. The old folks lived at Petersay, twenty-five miles to the southward. He had taken up a "claim" to carve his own home out of the woods at Fenebonk, and his grown sisters, Margat, staid and reliable, and Loo, bright and witty, were keeping house for him. Thorburn Alder was visiting them. He had just recovered from a severe illness and had been sent to rough it in the woods in hope of winning some of the vigor of his hosts. Their home was of unhewn logs, unfloored, and roofed with sods, which bore a luxuriant crop of grass and weeds. The primitive woods around were broken in two places: one where the roughest of roads led southward to Petersay; the other where the sparkling lake rolled on a pebbly shore and gave a glimpse of their nearest neighbor's house—four miles across the water.

Their daily round had little change. Corney was up at daybreak to light the fire, call his sisters, and feed the horses while they prepared breakfast. At six the meal was over and Corney went to his work. At noon, which Margat knew by the shadow of a certain rampike falling on the spring, a clear notification to draw fresh water for the table, Loo would hang a white rag on a pole, and Corney, seeing the signal, would return from summer fallow or hayfield, grimy, swarthy, and ruddy, a picture of manly vigor and honest toil. Thor might be away all day, but at night, when they again assembled at the table, he would come from lake or distant ridge and eat a supper like the dinner and breakfast, for meals as well as days were exact repeats: pork, bread, potatoes, and tea, with occasionally eggs supplied by a dozen hens around the little log stable, with, rarely, a variation of wild meat, for Thor was not a hunter and Corney had little time for anything but the farm.

II

THE LYNX

A huge four-foot basswood had gone the way of all trees. Death had been generous—

The Boy and the Lynx

had sent the three warnings: it was the biggest
of its kind, its children were grown up, it was
hollow. The wintry blast that sent it down
had broken it across and revealed a great hole
where should have been its heart. A long
wooden cavern in the middle of a sunny opening, it now lay, and presented an ideal home
for a Lynx when she sought a sheltered nesting-
place for her coming brood.

Old was she and gaunt, for this was a year
of hard times for the Lynxes. A Rabbit plague
the autumn before had swept away their main
support; a winter of deep snow and sudden
crusts had killed off nearly all the Partridges;
a long wet spring had destroyed the few growing coveys and had kept the ponds and streams
so full that Fish and Frogs were safe from their
armed paws, and this mother Lynx fared no
better than her kind.

The little ones—half starved before they
came—were a double drain, for they took the
time she might have spent in hunting.

The Northern Hare is the favorite food of
the Lynx, and in some years she could have
killed fifty in one day, but never one did she

The Boy and the Lynx

see this season. The plague had done its work too well.

One day she caught a Red-squirrel which had run into a hollow log that proved a trap. Another day a fetid Blacksnake was her only food. A day was missed, and the little ones whined piteously for their natural food and failing drink. One day she saw a large black animal of unpleasant but familiar smell. Swiftly and silently she sprang to make attack. She struck it once on the nose, but the Porcupine doubled his head under, his tail flew up, and the mother Lynx was speared in a dozen places with the little stinging javelins. She drew them all with her teeth, for she had "learned Porcupine" years before, and only the hard push of want would have made her strike one now.

A Frog was all she caught that day. On the next, as she ranged the farthest woods in a long, hard hunt, she heard a singular calling voice. It was new to her. She approached it cautiously, up wind, got many new odors and some more strange sounds in coming. The loud, clear, rolling call was repeated as the mother Lynx came to an opening in the forest.

174

One day she found a Porcupine.

The Boy and the Lynx

In the middle of it were two enormous musk-rat or beaver-houses, far bigger than the biggest she ever before had seen. They were made partly of logs and situated, not in a pond, but on a dry knoll. Walking about them were a number of Partridges, that is, birds like Partridges, only larger and of various colors, red, yellow, and white.

She quivered with the excitement that in a man would have been called buck-fever. Food—food—abundance of food, and the old huntress sank to earth. Her breast was on the ground, her elbows above her back, as she made stalk, her shrewdest, subtlest stalk ; one of those Partridges she must have at any price; no trick now must go untried, no error in this hunt; if it took hours—all day—she must approach with certainty to win before the quarry took to flight.

Only a few bounds it was from wood shelter to the great rat-house, but she was an hour in crawling that small space. From stump to brush, from log to bunch of grass she sneaked, a flattened form, and the Partridges saw her not. They fed about, the biggest uttering the ringing call that first had fallen on her ear.

177

The Boy and the Lynx

Once they seemed to sense their peril, but a long await dispelled the fear. Now they were almost in reach, and she trembled with all the eagerness of the hunting heart and the hungry maw. Her eye centred on a white one not quite the nearest, but the color seemed to hold her gaze.

There was an open space around the rat-house; outside that were tall weeds, and stumps were scattered everywhere. The white bird wandered behind these weeds, the red one of the loud voice flew to the top of the rat-mound and sang as before. The mother Lynx sank lower yet. It seemed an alarm note; but no, the white one still was there; she could see its feathers gleaming through the weeds. An open space now lay about. The huntress, flattened like an empty skin, trailed slow and silent on the ground behind a log no thicker than her neck; if she could reach that tuft of brush she could get unseen to the weeds and then would be near enough to spring. She could smell them now—the rich and potent smell of life, of flesh and blood, that set her limbs a-tingle and her eyes a-glow.

178

The Boy and the Lynx

The Partridges still scratched and fed; another flew to the high top, but the white one remained. Five more slow-gliding, silent steps, and the Lynx was behind the weeds, the white bird shining through; she gauged the distance, tried the footing, swung her hind legs to clear some fallen brush, then *leaped* direct with all her force, and the white one never knew the death it died, for the fateful gray shadow dropped, the swift and deadly did their work, and before the other birds could realize the foe or fly, the Lynx was gone, with the white bird squirming in her jaws.

Uttering an unnecessary growl of inborn ferocity and joy she bounded into the forest, and bee-like sped for home. The last quiver had gone from the warm body of the victim when she heard the sound of heavy feet ahead. She leaped on a log. The wings of her prey were muffling her eyes, so she laid the bird down and held it safely with one paw. The sound drew nearer, the bushes bent, and a Boy stepped into view. The old Lynx knew and hated his kind. She had watched them at night, had followed them, had been hunted and hurt by them. For

a moment they stood face to face. The huntress growled a warning that was also a chal-
lenge and a defiance, picked up the bird and
bounded from the log into the sheltering bushes.
It was a mile or two to the den, but she stayed
not to eat till the sunlit opening and the big
basswood came to view; then a low " prr—prr "
called forth the little ones to revel with their
mother in a plenteous meal of the choicest
food.

III

THE HOME OF THE LYNX

At first Thor, being town-bred, was timid
about venturing into the woods beyond the
sound of Corney's axe; but day by day he
went farther, guiding himself, not by unreliable
moss on trees, but by sun, compass, and land-
scape features. His purpose was to learn about
the wild animals rather than to kill them; but
the naturalist is close kin to the sportsman,
and the gun was his constant companion. In
the clearing, the only animal of any size was a
fat Woodchuck; it had a hole under a stump

The Boy and the Lynx

some hundred yards from the shanty. On
sunny mornings it used to lie basking on the
stump, but eternal vigilance is the price of
every good thing in the woods. The Woodchuck was always alert and Thor tried in vain
to shoot or even to trap him.

"Hyar," said Corney one morning, "time
we had some fresh meat." He took down his
rifle, an old-fashioned brass-mounted small-bore,
and loading with care that showed the true
rifleman, he steadied the weapon against the
door-jamb and fired. The Woodchuck fell
backward and lay still. Thor raced to the
place and returned in triumph with the animal,
shouting: "Plumb through the head—one hundred and twenty yards."

Corney controlled the gratified smile that
wrestled with the corners of his mouth, but his
bright eyes shone a trifle brighter for the moment.

It was no mere killing for killing's sake, for
the Woodchuck was spreading a belt of destruc-
tion in the crop around his den. Its flesh
supplied the family with more than one good
meal and Corney showed Thor how to use the

The Boy and the Lynx

skin. First the pelt was wrapped in hard-wood ashes for twenty-four hours. This brought the hair off. Then the skin was soaked for three days in soft soap and worked by hand, as it dried, till it came out a white strong leather.

Thor's wanderings extended farther in search of the things which always came as surprises however much he was looking for them. Many days were blanks and others would be crowded with incidents, for unexpectedness is above all the peculiar feature of hunting, and its lasting charm. One day he had gone far beyond the ridge in a new direction and passed through an open glade where lay the broken trunk of a huge basswood. The size impressed it on his memory. He swung past the glade to make for the lake, a mile to the west, and twenty minutes later he started back as his eye rested on a huge black animal in the crotch of a hemlock, some thirty feet from the ground. A Bear! At last, this was the test of nerve he had half expected all summer; had been wondering how that mystery " himself " would act under this very trial. He stood still; his right hand dived into his pocket and, bringing out three or

The Boy and the Lynx

four buckshot, which he carried for emergency,
he dropped them on top of the birdshot already
in the gun, then rammed a wad to hold them
down.

The Bear had not moved and the boy could
not see its head, but now he studied it carefully. It was not such a large one—no, it was
a small one, yes, very small—a cub. A cub!
That meant a mother Bear at hand, and Thor
looked about with some fear, but seeing no
signs of any except the little one, he levelled
the gun and fired.

Then to his surprise down crashed the animal quite dead; it was not a Bear, but a large
Porcupine. As it lay there he examined it with
wonder and regret, for he had no wish to kill
such a harmless creature. On its grotesque face
he found two or three long scratches which
proved that he had not been its only enemy.
As he turned away he noticed some blood on
his trousers, then saw that his left hand was
bleeding. He had wounded himself quite severely on the quills of the animal without knowing it. He was sorry to leave the specimen
there, and Loo, when she learned of it, said it

The Boy and the Lynx

was a shame not to skin it when she "needed
a fur-lined cape for the winter."

On another day Thor had gone without a
gun, as he meant only to gather some curious
plants he had seen. They were close to the
clearing; he knew the place by a fallen elm. As
he came to it he heard a peculiar sound. Then
on the log his eye caught two moving things.
He lifted a bough and got a clear view. They
were the head and tail of an enormous Lynx.
It had seen him and was glaring and grumbling;
and under its foot on the log was a white bird
that a second glance showed to be one of their
own precious hens. How fierce and cruel the
brute looked! How Thor hated it! and fairly
gnashed his teeth with disgust that now, when
his greatest chance was come, he for once was
without his gun. He was in not a little fear,
too, and stood wondering what to do. The
Lynx growled louder; its stumpy tail twitched
viciously for a minute, then it picked up its
victim, and leaping from the log was lost to
view.

As it was a very rainy summer, the ground
was soft everywhere, and the young hunter

The Boy and the Lynx

was led to follow tracks that would have defied
an expert in dryer times. One day he came on
piglike footprints in the woods. He followed
them with little difficulty, for they were new,
and a heavy rain two hours before had washed
out all other trails. After about half a mile
they led him to an open ravine, and as he
reached its brow he saw across it a flash of
white; then his keen young eyes made out the
forms of a Deer and a spotted Fawn gazing at
him curiously. Though on their trail he was
not a little startled. He gazed at them open-
mouthed. The mother turned and raised the
danger flag, her white tail, and bounded lightly
away, to be followed by the youngster, clearing low trunks with an effortless leap, or bend-
ing down with catlike suppleness when they
came to a log upraised so that they might pass
below.

He never again got a chance to shoot at
them, though more than once he saw the same
two tracks, or believed they were the same, as
for some cause never yet explained, Deer were
scarcer in that unbroken forest than they were
in later years when clearings spread around.

185

The Boy and the Lynx

He never again saw *them ;* but he saw the mother once—he thought it was the same— she was searching the woods with her nose, try- ing the ground for trails; she was nervous and anxious, evidently seeking. Thor remembered a trick that Corney had told him. He gently stooped, took up a broad blade of grass, laid it between the edges of his thumbs, then blowing through this simple squeaker he made a short, shrill bleat, a fair imitation of a Fawn's cry for the mother, and the Deer, though a long way off, came bounding toward him. He snatched his gun, meaning to kill her, but the movement caught her eye. She stopped. Her mane bristled a little; she sniffed and looked inquir- ingly at him. Her big soft eyes touched his heart, held back his hand; she took a cautious step nearer, got a full whiff of her mortal enemy, bounded behind a big tree and away before his merciful impulse was gone. "Poor thing," said Thor, "I believe she has lost her little one."

Yet once more the Boy met a Lynx in the woods. Half an hour after seeing the lonely Deer he crossed the long ridge that lay some

The Boy and the Lynx

miles north of the shanty. He had passed the
glade where the great basswood lay when a
creature like a big bob-tailed Kitten appeared
and looked innocently at him. His gun went
up, as usual, but the Kitten merely cocked its
head on one side and fearlessly surveyed him.
Then a second one that he had not noticed before began to play with the first, pawing at its
tail and inviting its brother to tussle.

Thor's first thought to shoot was stayed as he
watched their gambols, but the remembrance of
his feud with their race came back. He had
almost raised the gun when a fierce rumble
close at hand gave him a start, and there, not
ten feet from him, stood the old one, looking
big and fierce as a Tigress. It was surely folly
to shoot at the young ones now. The boy
nervously dropped some buckshot on the charge
while the snarling growl rose and fell, but before he was ready to shoot at her the old one
had picked up something that was by her feet;
the boy got a glimpse of rich brown with white
spots—the limp form of a newly killed Fawn.
Then she passed out of sight. The Kittens followed, and he saw her no more until the time

when, life against life, they were weighed in the balance together.

IV

THE TERROR OF THE WOODS

Six weeks had passed in daily routine when one day the young giant seemed unusually quiet as he went about. His handsome face was very sober and he sang not at all that morning.

He and Thor slept on a hay-bunk in one corner of the main room, and that night the Boy awakened more than once to hear his companion groaning and tossing in his sleep.

Corney arose as usual in the morning and fed the horses, but lay down again while the sisters got breakfast. He roused himself by an effort and went back to work, but came home early. He was trembling from head to foot. It was hot summer weather, but he could not be kept warm. After several hours a reaction set in and Corney was in a high fever. The family knew well now that he had the dreaded chills and fever of the backwoods. Margat went out

188

PIPSISSEWA

"There stood the Old One, . . . as fierce as a Tigress."

The Boy and the Lynx

and gathered a lapful of pipsissewa to make tea, of which Corney was encouraged to drink copiously.

But in spite of all their herbs and nursing the young man got worse. At the end of ten days he was greatly reduced in flesh and incapable of work, so on one of the " well days " that are usual in the course of the disease he said :

" Say, gurruls, I can't stand it no longer. ₁Guess I better go home. I 'm well enough to drive to-day, for a while anyway ; if I 'm took down I 'll lay in the wagon, and the horses will fetch me home. Mother 'll have me all right in a week or so. If you run out of grub before I come back take the canoe to Ellerton's."

So the girls harnessed the horses ; the wagon was partly filled with hay, and Corney, weak and white-faced, drove away on the long rough road, and left them feeling much as though they were on a desert island and their only boat had been taken from them.

Half a week had scarcely gone before all three of them, Margat, Loo, and Thor, were taken down with a yet more virulent form of chills and fever.

The Boy and the Lynx

Corney had had every other a "well day," but with these three there were no "well days" and the house became an abode of misery.

Seven days passed, and now Margat could not leave her bed and Loo was barely able to walk around the house. She was a brave girl with a fund of drollery which did much toward keeping up all their spirits, but her merriest jokes fell ghastly from her wan, pinched face. Thor, though weak and ill, was the strongest and did for the others, cooking and serving each day a simple meal, for they could eat very little, fortunately, perhaps, as there was very little, and Corney could not return for another week.

Soon Thor was the only one able to rise, and one morning when he dragged himself to cut the little usual slice of their treasured bacon he found, to his horror, that the whole piece was gone. It had been stolen, doubtless by some wild animal, from the little box on the shady side of the house, where it was kept safe from flies. Now they were down to flour and tea. He was in despair, when his eye lighted on the Chickens about the stable; but what 's the use?

The Boy and the Lynx

In his feeble state he might as well try to catch
a Deer or a Hawk.   Suddenly he remembered
his gun and very soon was preparing a fat Hen
for the pot.   He boiled it whole as the easiest
way to cook it, and the broth was the first really
tempting food they had had for some time.

They kept alive for three wretched days on
that Chicken, and when it was finished Thor
again took down his gun—it seemed a much
heavier gun now.   He crawled to the barn, but
he was so weak and shaky that he missed several times before he brought down a fowl.
Corney had taken the rifle away with him and
three charges of gun ammunition were all that
now remained.

Thor was surprised to see how few Hens there
were now, only three or four.   There used to
be over a dozen.   Three days later he made
another raid.   He saw but one Hen and he
used up his last ammunition to get that.

His daily routine now was a monotony of
horror.   In the morning, which was his " well
time," he prepared a little food for the house-
hold and got ready for the night of raging fever
by putting a bucket of water on a block at the

193

The Boy and the Lynx

head of each bunk. About one o'clock, with fearful regularity, the chills would come on, with trembling from head to foot and chattering teeth, and cold, cold, within and without. Nothing seemed to give any warmth—fire seemed to have lost its power. There was nothing to do but to lie and shake and suffer all the slow torture of freezing to death and shaking to pieces. For six hours it would keep up, and to the torture, nausea lent its horrid aid throughout; then about seven or eight o'clock in the evening a change would come; a burning fever set in; no ice could have seemed cool to him then; water—water—was all he craved, and drank and drank until three or four in the morning, when the fever would abate, and a sleep of total exhaustion followed.

"If you run out of food take the canoe to Ellerton's," was the brother's last word. Who was to take the canoe?

There was but half a Chicken now between them and starvation, and no sign of Corney.

For three interminable weeks the deadly program dragged along. It went on the same yet worse, as the sufferers grew weaker—a few

The Boy and the Lynx

days more and the Boy also would be unable to leave his couch. Then what ?

Despair was on the house and the silent cry of each was, " Oh, God! will Corney never come ? "

V

THE HOME OF THE BOY

On the day of that last Chicken, Thor was all morning carrying water enough for the coming three fevers. The chill attacked him sooner than it was due and his fever was worse than ever before.

He drank deeply and often from the bucket at his head. He had filled it, and it was nearly emptied when about two in the morning the fever left him and he fell asleep.

In the gray dawn he was awakened by a curious sound not far away—a splashing of water. He turned his head to see two glaring eyes within a foot of his face—a great Beast lapping the water in the bucket by his bed.

Thor gazed in horror for a moment, then closed his eyes, sure that he was dreaming,

The Boy and the Lynx

certain that this was a nightmare of India with a Tiger by his couch; but the lapping continued. He looked up; yes, it still was there. He tried to find his voice but uttered only a gurgle. The great furry head quivered, a sniff came from below the shining eyeballs, and the creature, whatever it was, dropped to its front feet and went across the hut under the table. Thor was fully awake now; he rose slowly on his elbow and feebly shouted "Sssh-hi," at which the shining eyes reappeared under the table and the gray form came forth. Calmly it walked across the ground and glided under the lowest log at a place where an old potato-pit left an opening and disappeared.

What was it? The sick boy hardly knew—some savage Beast of prey, undoubtedly. He was totally unnerved. He shook with fear and a sense of helplessness, and the night passed in fitful sleep and sudden starts awake to search the gloom again for those fearful eyes and the great gray gliding form. In the morning he did not know whether it were not all a delirium, yet he made a feeble effort to close the old cellar hole with some firewood.

196

The Boy and the Lynx

The three had little appetite, but even that they restrained since now they were down to part of a Chicken, and Corney, evidently he supposed they had been to Ellerton's and got all the food they needed.

Again that night, when the fever left him weak and dozing, Thor was awakened by a noise in the room, a sound of crunching bones. He looked around to see dimly outlined against the little window, the form of a large animal on the table. Thor shouted; he tried to hurl his boot at the intruder. It leaped lightly to the ground and passed out of the hole, again wide open.

It was no dream this time, he knew, and the women knew it, too; not only had they heard the creature, but the Chicken, the last of their food, was wholly gone.

Poor Thor barely left his couch that day. It needed all the querulous complaints of the sick women to drive him forth. Down by the spring he found a few berries and divided them with the others. He made his usual preparations for the chills and the thirst, but he added this—by the side of his couch he put an old fish-spear—the only weapon he could find, now the gun was useless—a pine-root candle and some matches. He knew the Beast was coming back again—was coming hungry. It would find no food; what more natural, he thought, than take the living prey lying there so helpless? And a vision came of the limp brown form of the little Fawn, borne off in those same cruel jaws.

Once again he barricaded the hole with firewood, and the night passed as usual, but without any fierce visitor. Their food that day was flour and water, and to cook it Thor was forced to use some of his barricade. Loo attempted some feeble joke, guessed she was light enough to fly now and tried to rise, but she got no farther than the edge of the bunk. The same preparations were made, and the night wore on, but early in the morning, Thor was again awakened rudely by the sound of lapping water by his bed, and there, as before, were the glowing eyeballs, the great head, the gray form relieved by the dim light from the dawning window.

Thor put all his strength into what was

The Boy and the Lynx

meant for a bold shout, but it was merely a
feeble screech. He rose slowly and called out:
" Loo, Margat!   The Lynx—here's the Lynx
again ! "

" May God help ye, for we can't," was the
answer.

" Sssh-hi! "   Thor tried again to drive the
Beast away.   It leaped on to the table by the
window and stood up growling under the useless gun.   Thor thought it was going to leap
through the glass as it faced the window a
moment; but it turned and glared toward the
Boy, for he could see both eyes shining.   He
rose slowly to the side of his bunk and he
prayed for help, for he felt it was kill or be
killed.   He struck a match and lighted his
pine-root candle, held that in his left hand and
in his right took the old fish-spear, meaning to
fight, but he was so weak he had to use the
fish-spear as a crutch.   The great Beast stood
on the table still, but was crouching a little as
though for a spring.   Its eyes glowed red in
the torchlight.   Its short tail was switching from
side to side and its growling took a higher pitch.
Thor's knees were smiting together, but he

The Boy and the Lynx

levelled the spear and made a feeble lunge toward the brute. It sprang at the same moment, not at him, as he first thought—the torch and the boy's bold front had had effect—it went over his head to drop on the ground beyond and at once to slink under the bunk.

This was only a temporary repulse. Thor set the torch on a ledge of the logs, then took the spear in both hands. He was fighting for his life, and he knew it. He heard the voices of the women feebly praying. He saw only the glowing eyes under the bed and heard the growling in higher pitch as the Beast was nearing action. He steadied himself by a great effort and plunged the spear with all the force he could give it.

It struck something softer than the logs: a hideous snarl came forth. The boy threw all his weight on the weapon; the Beast was struggling to get at him; he felt its teeth and claws grating on the handle, and in spite of himself it was coming on; its powerful arms and claws were reaching for him now; he could not hold out long. He put on all his force, just a little more it was than before; the Beast lurched,

He made a feeble lunge at the Brute.

The Boy and the Lynx

there was a growling, a crack, and a sudden yielding; the rotten old spear-head had broken off, the Beast sprang out—at him—past him— never touched him, but across through the hole and away, to be seen no more.

Thor fell on the bed and lost all consciousness.

He lay there he knew not how long, but was awakened in broad daylight by a loud, cheery voice:

"Hello! Hello!—are ye all dead? Loo! Thor! Margat!"

He had no strength to answer, but there was a trampling of horses outside, a heavy step, the door was forced open, and in strode Corney, handsome and hearty as ever. But what a flash of horror and pain came over his face on entering the silent shanty!

"Dead?" he gasped. "Who's dead— where are you? Thor?" Then, "Who is it? Loo? Margat?"

"Corney—Corney," came feebly from the bunk. "They're in there. They're awful sick. We have nothing to eat."

"Oh, what a fool I be!" said Corney again

203

and again. "I made sure ye 'd go to Ellerton's and get all ye wanted."

"We had no chance, Corney; we were all three brought down at once, right after you left. Then the Lynx came and cleared up the Hens, and all in the house, too."

"Well, ye got even with her," and Corney pointed to the trail of blood across the mud floor and out under the logs.

Good food, nursing, and medicine restored them all.

A month or two later, when the women wanted a new leaching-barrel, Thor said: "I know where there is a hollow basswood as big as a hogshead."

He and Corney went to the place, and when they cut off what they needed, they found in the far end of it the dried-up bodies of two little Lynxes with that of the mother, and in the side of the old one was the head of a fish-spear broken from the handle.

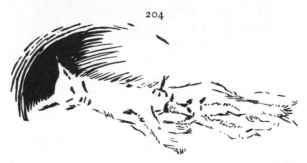

Little Warhorse

Little Warhorse
The History of a Jack-rabbit

I

HE Little Warhorse knew practically all the Dogs in town. First, there was a very large brown Dog that had pursued him many times, a Dog that he always got rid of by slipping through a hole in a board fence. Second, there was a small active Dog that could follow through that hole, and him he baffled by leaping a twenty-foot irrigation ditch that had steep sides and a swift current. The Dog could not make this leap. It was "sure medicine" for that foe, and the boys still call the place "Old

Jacky's Jump." But there was a Greyhound
that could leap better than the Jack, and when
he could not follow through a fence, he jumped
over it. He tried the Warhorse's mettle more
than once, and Jacky only saved himself by his
quick dodging, till they got to an Osage hedge,
and here the Greyhound had to give it up. Besides these, there was in town a rabble of big
and little Dogs that were troublesome, but
easily left behind in the open.

In the country there was a Dog at each
farm-house, but only one that the Warhorse
really feared; that was a long-legged, fierce,
black Dog, a brute so swift and pertinacious
that he had several times forced the Warhorse
almost to the last extremity.

For the town Cats he cared little; only once
or twice had he been threatened by them. A
huge Tom-cat flushed with many victories came
crawling up to where he fed one moonlight
night. Jack Warhorse saw the black creature
with the glowing eyes, and a moment before
the final rush, he faced it, raised up on his
haunches,—his hind legs,—at full length on his
toes,—with his broad ears towering up yet six

208

Little Warhorse

inches higher; then letting out a loud *churrr-churrr*, his best attempt at a roar, he sprang five feet forward and landed on the Cat's head, driving in his sharp hind nails, and the old Tom fled in terror from the weird two-legged giant. This trick he had tried several times with success, but twice it turned out a sad failure: once, when the Cat proved to be a mother whose Kittens were near; then Jack Warhorse had to flee for his life; and the other time was when he made the mistake of landing hard on a Skunk.

But the Greyhound was the dangerous enemy, and in him the Warhorse might have found his fate, but for a curious adventure with a happy ending for Jack.

He fed by night; there were fewer enemies about then, and it was easier to hide; but one day at dawn in winter he had lingered long at an alfalfa stack and was crossing the open snow toward his favorite form, when, as ill-luck would have it, he met the Greyhound prowling outside the town. With open snow and growing daylight there was no chance to hide, nothing but a run in the open with soft snow

that hindered the Jack more than it did the
Hound.

Off they went—superb runners in fine
fettle. How they skimmed across the snow,
raising it in little *puff—puff—puffs*, each time
their nimble feet went down. This way and
that, swerving and dodging, went the chase.
Everything favored the Dog,—his empty
stomach, the cold weather, the soft snow,—
while the Rabbit was handicapped by his
heavy meal of alfalfa. But his feet went *puff*
—puff so fast that a dozen of the little snow-
jets were in view at once. The chase continued in the open; no friendly hedge was near,
and every attempt to reach a fence was cleverly stopped by the Hound. Jack's ears were
losing their bold up-cock, a sure sign of failing
heart or wind, when all at once these flags went
stiffly up, as under sudden renewal of strength.
The Warhorse put forth all his power, not to
reach the hedge to the north, but over the open
prairie eastward. The Greyhound followed,
and within fifty yards the Jack dodged to foil
his fierce pursuer; but on the next tack he was
on his eastern course again, and so tacking

and dodging, he kept the line direct for the
next farm-house, where was a very high board
fence with a hen-hole, and where also there
dwelt his other hated enemy, the big black
Dog. An outer hedge delayed the Greyhound
for a moment and gave Jack time to dash
through the hen-hole into the yard, where he
hid to one side. The Greyhound rushed
around to the low gate, leaped over that among
the Hens, and as they fled cackling and fluttering, some Lambs bleated loudly. Their natural
guardian, the big black Dog, ran to the rescue,
and Warhorse slipped out again by the hole
at which he had entered. Horrible sounds of
Dog hate and fury were heard behind him in
the hen-yard, and soon the shouts of men were
added. How it ended he did not know or seek
to learn, but it was remarkable that he never
afterward was troubled by the swift Greyhound
that formerly lived in Newchusen.

II

Hard times and easy times had long followed
in turn and been taken as matters of course;

but recent years in the State of Kaskado had brought to the Jack-rabbits a succession of remarkable ups and downs. In the old days they had their endless fight with Birds and Beasts of Prey, with cold and heat, with pestilence and with flies whose sting bred a loathsome disease, and yet had held their own. But the settling of the country by farmers made many changes.

Dogs and guns arriving in numbers reduced the ranks of Coyotes, Foxes, Wolves, Badgers, and Hawks that preyed on the Jack, so that in a few years the Rabbits were multiplied in great swarms; but now Pestilence broke out and swept them away. Only the strongest—the double-seasoned—remained. For a while a Jack-rabbit was a rarity; but during this time another change came in. The Osage-orange hedges planted everywhere afforded a new refuge, and now the safety of a Jack-rabbit was less often his speed than his wits, and the wise ones, when pursued by a Dog or Coyote, would rush to the nearest hedge through a small hole and escape while the enemy sought for a larger one by which to follow. The Coy-

Little Warhorse

otes rose to this and developed the trick of the relay chase. In this one Coyote takes one field, another the next, and if the Rabbit attempts the "hedge-ruse" they work from each side and usually win their prey. The Rabbit remedy for this, is keen eyes to see the second Coyote, avoidance of that field, then good legs to distance the first enemy.

Thus the Jack-rabbits, after being successively numerous, scarce, in myriads, and rare, were now again on the increase, and those which survived, selected by a hundred hard trials, were enabled to flourish where their ancestors could not have outlived a single season.

Their favorite grounds were, not the broad open stretches of the big ranches, but the complicated, much-fenced fields of the farms, where these were so small and close as to be like a big straggling village.

One of these vegetable villages had sprung up around the railway station of Newchusen. The country a mile away was well supplied with Jack-rabbits of the new and selected stock. Among them was a little lady Rabbit

213

Little Warhorse

called "Bright-eyes," from her leading characteristic as she sat gray in the gray brush. She was a good runner, but was especially successful with the fence-play that baffled the Coyotes. She made her nest out in an open pasture, an untouched tract of the ancient prairie. Here her brood were born and raised. One like herself was bright-eyed, in coat of silver-gray, and partly gifted with her ready wits, but in the other, there appeared a rare combination of his mother's gifts with the best that was in the best strain of the new Jack-rabbits of the plains.

This was the one whose adventures we have been following, the one that later on the turf won the name of Little Warhorse and that afterward achieved a world-wide fame.

Ancient tricks of his kind he revived and put to new uses, and ancient enemies he learned to fight with new-found tricks.

When a mere baby he discovered a plan that was worthy of the wisest Rabbit in Kaskado. He was pursued by a horrible little Yellow Dog, and he had tried in vain to get rid of him by dodging among the fields and

Little Warhorse

farms. This is good play against a Coyote, because the farmers and the Dogs will often help
the Jack, without knowing it, by attacking the
Coyote. But now the plan did not work at
all, for the little Dog managed to keep after
him through one fence after another, and Jack
Warhorse, not yet full-grown, much less sea-
soned, was beginning to feel the strain. His
ears were no longer up straight, but angling
back and at times drooping to a level, as he
darted through a very little hole in an Osage
hedge, only to find that his nimble enemy had
done the same without loss of time. In the
middle of the field was a small herd of cattle
and with them a calf.

There is in wild animals a curious impulse to
trust any stranger when in desperate straits.
The foe behind they know means death.
There is just a chance, and the only one left, that
the stranger may prove friendly ; and it was this
last desperate chance that drew Jack Warhorse
to the Cows.

It is quite sure that the Cows would have
stood by in stolid indifference so far as the
Rabbit was concerned, but they have a deep-

215

rooted hatred of a Dog, and when they saw the Yellow Cur coming bounding toward them, their tails and noses went up; they sniffed angrily, then closed up ranks, and led by the Cow that owned the Calf, they charged at the Dog, while Jack took refuge under a low thorn-bush. The Dog swerved aside to attack the Calf, at least the old Cow thought he did, and she followed him so fiercely that he barely escaped from that field with his life.

It was a good old plan—one that doubtless came from the days when Buffalo and Coyote played the parts of Cow and Dog. Jack never forgot it, and more than once it saved his life.

In color as well as in power he was a rarity.

Animals are colored in one or other of two general plans: one that matches them with their surroundings and helps them to hide— this is called "protective"; the other that makes them very visible for several purposes— this is called "directive." Jack-rabbits are peculiar in being painted both ways. As they squat in their form in the gray brush or clods, they are soft gray on their ears, head, back, and

216

sides; they match the ground and cannot be seen until close at hand—they are *protectively* colored. But the moment it is clear to the Jack that the approaching foe will find him, he jumps up and dashes away. He throws off all disguise now, the gray seems to disappear; he makes a lightning change, and his ears show snowy white with black tips, the legs are white, his tail is a black spot in a blaze of white. He is a black-and-white Rabbit now. His coloring is all *directive*. How is it done? Very simply. The front side of the ear is gray, the back, black and white. The black tail with its white halo, and the legs, are tucked below. He is sitting on them. The gray mantle is pulled down and enlarged as he sits, but when he jumps up it shrinks somewhat, all his black-and-white marks are now shown, and just as his colors formerly whispered, " I am a clod," they now shout aloud, " I am a Jack-rabbit."

Why should he do this? Why should a timid creature running for his life thus proclaim to all the world his name instead of trying to hide? There must be some good reason. It must pay, or the Rabbit would never have done it. The answer is, if the creature that scared him up was one of his own kind—i.e., this was a false alarm—then at once, by showing his national colors, the mistake is made right. On the other hand, if it be a Coyote, Fox, or Dog, they see at once, this is a Jack-rabbit, and know that it would be waste of time for them to pursue him. They say in effect, "This is a Jack-rabbit, and I cannot catch a Jack in open race." They give it up, and that, of course, saves the Jack a great deal of unnecessary running and worry. The black-and-white spots are the national uniform and flag of the Jacks. In poor specimens they are apt to be dull, but in the finest specimens they are not only larger, but brighter than usual, and the Little Warhorse, gray when he sat in his form, blazed like charcoal and snow, when he flung his defiance to the Fox and buff Coyote, and danced with little effort before them, first a black-and-white Jack, then a little white spot, and last a speck of thistledown, before the distance swallowed him.

Many of the farmers' Dogs had learned the lesson: "A grayish Rabbit you may catch, but

Little Warhorse

a very black-and-white one is hopeless." They might, indeed, follow for a time, but that was merely for the fun of a chivvy, and his growing power often led Warhorse to seek the chase for the sake of a little excitement, and to take hazards that others less gifted were most careful to avoid.

Jack, like all other wild animals, had a certain range or country which was home to him, and outside of this he rarely strayed. It was about three miles across, extending easterly from the centre of the village. Scattered through this he had a number of "forms," or "beds" as they are locally called. These were mere hollows situated under a sheltering bush or bunch of grass, without lining excepting the accidental grass and in-blown leaves. But comfort was not forgotten. Some of them were for hot weather; they faced the north, were scarcely sunk, were little more than shady places. Some for the cold weather were deep hollows with southern exposure, and others for the wet were well roofed with herbage and faced the west. In one or other of these he spent the day, and at night he went forth to

feed with his kind, sporting and romping on the moonlight nights like a lot of puppy Dogs, but careful to be gone by sunrise, and safely tucked in a bed that was suited to the weather.

The safest ground for the Jacks was among the farms, where not only Osage hedges, but also the newly arrived barb-wire, made hurdles and hazards in the path of possible enemies. But the finest of the forage is nearer to the village among the truck-farms—the finest of forage and the fiercest of dangers. Some of the dangers of the plains were lacking, but the greater perils of men, guns, Dogs, and impassable fences are much increased. Yet those who knew Warhorse best were not at all surprised to find that he had made a form in the middle of a market-gardener's melon-patch. A score of dangers beset him here, but there was also a score of unusual delights and a score of holes in the fence for times when he had to fly, with at least twoscore of expedients to help him afterward.

Little Warhorse

III

Newchusen was a typical Western town. Everywhere in it, were to be seen strenuous efforts at uglification, crowned with unmeasured success. The streets were straight level lanes without curves or beauty-spots. The houses were cheap and mean structures of flimsy boards and tar paper, and not even honest in their ugliness, for each of them was pretending to be something better than itself. One had a false front to make it look like two stories, another was of imitation brick, a third pretended to be a marble temple.

But all agreed in being the ugliest things ever used as human dwellings, and in each could be read the owner's secret thought—to stand it for a year or so, then move out somewhere else. The only beauties of the place, and those unintentional, were the long lines of hand-planted shade-trees, uglified as far as possible with whitewashed trunks and croppy heads, but still lovable, growing, living things.

The only building in town with a touch of

picturesqueness was the grain elevator. It was not posing as a Greek temple or a Swiss châlet, but simply a strong, rough, honest, grain elevator. At the end of each street was a vista of the prairie, with its farm-houses, windmill pumps, and long lines of Osage-orange hedges.  Here at least was something of interest—the gray-green hedges, thick, sturdy, and high, were dotted with their golden mock-oranges, useless fruit, but more welcome here than rain in a desert; for these balls were things of beauty, and swung on their long tough boughs they formed with the soft green leaves a color-chord that pleased the weary eye.

Such a town is a place to get out of, as soon as possible, so thought the traveller who found himself laid over here for two days in late winter. He asked after the sights of the place. A white Muskrat stuffed in a case "down to the saloon"; old Baccy Bullin, who had been scalped by the Indians forty years ago; and a pipe once smoked by Kit Carson, proved unattractive, so he turned toward the prairie, still white with snow.

A mark among the numerous Dog tracks

Little Warhorse

caught his eye: it was the track of a large
Jack-rabbit. He asked a passer-by if there
were any Rabbits in town.
"No, I reckon not. I never seen none,"
was the answer. A mill-hand gave the same
reply, but a small boy with a bundle of newspapers said: "You bet there is; there 's lots
of them out there on the prairie, and they come
in town a-plenty. Why, there 's a big, big
feller lives right round Si Kalb's melon-patch—
oh, an awful big feller, and just as black and
as white as checkers!" and thus he sent the
stranger eastward on his walk.

The "big, big, awful big one" was the Little
Warhorse himself. He did n't live in Kalb's
melon-patch; he was there only at odd times.
He was not there now; he was in his west-
fronting form or bed, because a raw east wind
was setting in. It was due east of Madison
Avenue, and as the stranger plodded that way
the Rabbit watched him. As long as the man
kept the road the Jack was quiet, but the road
turned shortly to the north, and the man by
chance left it and came straight on. Then
the Jack saw trouble ahead. The moment the

Little Warhorse

man left the beaten track, he bounded from
his form, and wheeling, he sailed across the
prairie due east.

A Jack-rabbit running from its enemy ordi-
narily covers eight or nine feet at a bound, and
once in five or six bounds, it makes an observation hop, leaping not along, but high in the air,
so as to get above all herbage and bushes and
take in the situation. A silly young Jack will
make an observation hop as often as one in
four, and so waste a great deal of time. A
clever Jack will make one hop in eight or nine,
do for observation. But Jack Warhorse as he
sped, got all the information he needed, in one
hop out of a dozen, while ten to fourteen feet
were covered by each of his flying bounds. Yet
another personal peculiarity showed in the
trail he left. When a Cottontail or a Wood-
hare runs, his tail is curled up tight on his
back, and does not touch the snow. When a
Jack runs, his tail hangs downward or backward, with the tip curved or straight, according
to the individual; in some, it points straight
down, and so, often leaves a little stroke
behind the foot-marks. The Warhorse's tail

The Warhorse doing a Spy-hop.

Little Warhorse

of shining black, was of unusual length, and at every bound, it left in the snow, a long stroke, so long that that alone was almost enough to tell which Rabbit had made the track.

Now some Rabbits seeing only a man without any Dog would have felt little fear, but Warhorse, remembering some former stinging experiences with a far-killer, fled when the foe was seventy-five yards away, and skimming low, he ran southeast to a fence that ran easterly. Behind this he went like a low-flying Hawk, till a mile away he reached another of his beds; and here, after an observation taken as he stood on his heels, he settled again to rest.

But not for long. In twenty minutes his great megaphone ears, so close to the ground, caught a regular sound—crunch, crunch, crunch—the tramp of a human foot, and he started up to see the man with the shining stick in his hand, now drawing near.

Warhorse bounded out and away for the fence. Never once did he rise to a "spy-hop" till the wire and rails were between him and his foe, an unnecessary precaution as it chanced, for the man was watching the trail and saw nothing of the Rabbit.

Jack skimmed along, keeping low and looking out for other enemies. He knew now that the man was on his track, and the old instinct born of ancestral trouble with Weasels was doubtless what prompted him to do the double trail. He ran in a long, straight course to a distant fence, followed its far side for fifty yards, then doubling back he retraced his trail and ran off in a new direction till he reached another of his dens or forms. He had been out all night and was very ready to rest, now that the sun was ablaze on the snow; but he had hardly got the place a little warmed when the "tramp, tramp, tramp" announced the enemy, and he hurried away.

After a half-a-mile run he stopped on a slight rise and marked the man still following, so he made a series of wonderful quirks in his trail, a succession of blind zigzags that would have puzzled most trailers; then running a hundred yards past a favorite form, he returned to it from the other side, and settled to rest, sure that now the enemy would be finally thrown off the scent.

Little Warhorse

It was slower than before, but still it came—
"tramp, tramp, tramp."

Jack awoke, but sat still. The man tramped
by on the trail one hundred yards in front of
him, and as he went on, Jack sprang out unseen, realizing that this was an unusual occasion needing a special effort. They had gone
in a vast circle around the home range of the
Warhorse and now were less than a mile from
the farm-house of the black Dog. There was
that wonderful board fence with the happily
planned hen-hole. It was a place of good
memory—here more than once he had won,
here especially he had baffled the Greyhound.

These doubtless were the motive thoughts
rather than any plan of playing one enemy
against another, and Warhorse bounded openly
across the snow to the fence of the big black
Dog.

The hen-hole was shut, and Warhorse, not a
little puzzled, sneaked around to find another,
without success, until, around the front, here
was the gate wide open, and inside lying on
some boards was the big Dog, fast asleep.
The Hens were sitting hunched up in the warm-

229

est corner of the yard. The house Cat was gingerly picking her way from barn to kitchen, as Warhorse halted in the gateway.

The black form of his pursuer was crawling down the far white prairie slope. Jack hopped quietly into the yard. A long-legged Rooster, that ought to have minded his own business, uttered a loud cackle as he saw the Rabbit hopping near. The Dog lying in the sun raised his head and stood up, and Jack's peril was dire. He squatted low and turned himself into a gray clod. He did it cleverly, but still might have been lost but for the Cat. Unwittingly, unwillingly, she saved him. The black Dog had taken three steps toward the Warhorse, though he did not know the Rabbit was there, and was now blocking the only way of escape from the yard, when the Cat came round the corner of the house, and leaping to a window-ledge brought a flower-pot rolling down. By that single awkward act she disturbed the armed neutrality existing between herself and the Dog. She fled to the barn, and of course a flying foe is all that is needed to send a Dog on the war-path. They passed within

thirty feet of the crouching Rabbit. As soon
as they were well gone, Jack turned, and without even a "Thank you, Pussy," he fled to the
open and away on the hard-beaten road.

The Cat had been rescued by the lady of
the house; the Dog was once more sprawling
on the boards when the man on Jack's trail
arrived. He carried, not a gun, but a stout
stick, sometimes called "dog-medicine," and
that was all that prevented the Dog attacking
the enemy of his prey.

This seemed to be the end of the trail. The
trick, whether planned or not, was a success,
and the Rabbit got rid of his troublesome fol-
lower.

Next day the stranger made another search
for the Jack and found, not himself, but his
track. He knew it by its tail-mark, its long
leaps and few spy-hops, but with it and running by it was the track of a smaller Rabbit.
Here is where they met, here they chased each
other in play, for no signs of battle were there
to be seen; here they fed or sat together in the
sun, there they ambled side by side, and here
again they sported in the snow, always to-

gether. There was only one conclusion: this was the mating season. This was a pair of Jack-rabbits—the Little Warhorse and his mate.

IV

Next summer was a wonderful year for the Jack-rabbits. A foolish law had set a bounty on Hawks and Owls and had caused a general massacre of these feathered policemen. Consequently the Rabbits had multiplied in such numbers that they now were threatening to devastate the country.

The farmers, who were the sufferers from the bounty law, as well as the makers of it, decided on a great Rabbit drive. All the county was invited to come, on a given morning, to the main road north of the county, with the intention of sweeping the whole region up-wind and at length driving the Rabbits into a huge corral of close wire netting. Dogs were barred as unmanageable, and guns as dangerous in a crowd; but every man and boy carried a couple of long sticks and a bag full of stones. Women came on horseback and in buggies;

232

many carried rattles or horns and tins to make
a noise. A number of the buggies trailed a
string of old cans or tied laths to scrape on the
wheel-spokes, and thus add no little to the
deafening clatter of the drive. As Rabbits
have marvellously sensitive hearing, a noise
that is distracting to mankind, is likely to prove
bewildering to them.

The weather was right, and at eight in the
morning the word to advance was given. The
line was about five miles long at first, and there
was a man or a boy every thirty or forty yards.
The buggies and riders kept perforce almost
entirely to the roads; but the beaters were
supposed, as a point of honor, to face everything, and keep the front unbroken. The advance was roughly in three sides of a square.
Each man made as much noise as he could, and
threshed every bush in his path. A number of
Rabbits hopped out. Some made for the lines,
to be at once assailed by a shower of stones that
laid many of them low. One or two did get
through and escaped, but the majority were
swept before the drive. At first the number seen
was small, but before three miles were covered

the Rabbits were running ahead in every direction. After five miles—and that took about three hours—the word for the wings to close in was given. The space between the men was shortened up till they were less than ten feet apart, and the whole drive converged on the corral with its two long guide wings or fences; the end lines joined these wings, and the surround was complete. The drivers marched rapidly now; scores of the Rabbits were killed as they ran too near the beaters. Their bodies strewed the ground, but the swarms seemed to increase; and in the final move, before the victims were cooped up in the corral, the two-acre space surrounded was a whirling throng of skurrying, jumping, bounding Rabbits. Round and round they circled and leaped, looking for a chance to escape; but the inexorable crowd grew thicker as the ring grew steadily smaller, and the whole swarm was forced along the chute into the tight corral, some to squat stupidly in the middle, some to race round the outer wall, some to seek hiding in corners or under each other.

And the Little Warhorse—where was he in all this ? The drive had swept him along, and

Little Warhorse

he had been one of the first to enter the corral.
But a curious plan of selection had been established. The pen was to be a death-trap for the
Rabbits, except the best, the soundest. And
many were there that were unsound; those that
think of all wild animals as pure and perfect
things, would have been shocked to see how
many halt, maimed, and diseased there were in
that pen of four thousand or five thousand
Jack-rabbits.

It was a Roman victory—the rabble of prisoners was to be butchered. The choicest were
to be reserved for the arena. The arena ? Yes,
that is the Coursing Park.

In that corral trap, prepared beforehand for
the Rabbits, were a number of small boxes
along the wall, a whole series of them, five
hundred at least, each large enough to hold
one Jack.

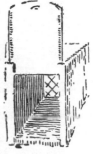

In the last rush of driving, the swiftest
Jacks got first to the pen. Some were swift
and silly; when once inside they rushed wildly
round and round. Some were swift and wise;
they quickly sought the hiding afforded by the
little boxes; all of these were now full. Thus

five hundred of the swiftest and wisest had been selected, in, not by any means an infallible way, but the simplest and readiest. These five hundred were destined to be coursed by Greyhounds. The surging mass of over four thousand were ruthlessly given to slaughter.

Five hundred little boxes with five hundred bright-eyed Jack-rabbits were put on the train that day, and among them was Little Jack Warhorse.

V

Rabbits take their troubles lightly, and it is not to be supposed that any great terror was felt by the boxed Jacks, once the uproar of the massacre was over; and when they reached the Coursing Park near the great city and were turned out one by one, very gently,—yes, gently; the Roman guards were careful of their prisoners, being responsible for them,—the Jacks found little to complain of, a big inclosure with plenty of good food, and no enemies to annoy them.

The very next morning their training began. A score of hatchways were opened into a

Little Warhorse

much larger field—the Park. After a number
of Jacks had wandered out through these doors
a rabble of boys appeared and drove them
back, pursuing them noisily until all were again
in the smaller field, called the Haven. A few
days of this taught the Jack-rabbits that when
pursued their safety was to get back by one of
the hatches into the Haven.

Now the second lesson began. The whole
band were driven out of a side door into a long
lane which led around three sides of the Park
to another inclosure at the far end. This was
the Starting Pen. Its door into the arena—that
is, the Park—was opened, the Rabbits driven
forth, and then a mob of boys and Dogs in
hiding, burst forth and pursued them across the
open. The whole army went bobbing and
bounding away, some of the younger ones
soaring in a spy-hop, as a matter of habit; but
low skimming ahead of them all was a gorgeous black-and-white one; clean-limbed and
bright-eyed, he had attracted attention in the
pen, but now in the field he led the band with
easy lope that put him as far ahead of them all as
they were ahead of the rabble of common Dogs.

Little Warhorse

" Luk at thot, would ye—but ain't he a Little
Warhorse?" shouted a villainous-looking Irish
stable-boy, and thus he was named. When half-
way across the course the Jacks remembered
the Haven, and all swept toward it and in like a
snow-cloud over the drifts.

This was the second lesson—to lead straight
for the Haven as soon as driven from the Pen.
In a week all had learned it, and were ready for
the great opening meet of the Coursing Club.

The Little Warhorse was now well known to
the grooms and hangers-on ; his colors usually
marked him clearly, and his leadership was in
a measure recognized by the long-eared herd
that fled with him. He figured more or less
with the Dogs in the talk and betting of the
men.

"Wonder if old Dignam is going to enter
Minkie this year? "

" Faix, an' if he does I bet the Little Warrhorrse will take the gimp out av her an' her
runnin' mate."

" I 'll bet three to one that my old Jen will
pick the Warhorse up before he passes the
grand stand," growled a dog-man.

Little Warhorse

" An' it 's meself will take thot bet in dollars,"
said Mickey, " an', moore than thot, Oi 'll put up
a hull month's stuff thot there ain't a dog in
the mate thot kin turrn the Warrhorrse oncet on
the hull coorse."

So they wrangled and wagered, but each day,
as they put the Rabbits through their paces,
there were more of those who believed that
they had found a wonderful runner in the Warhorse, one that would give the best Greyhounds
something that is rarely seen, a straight stern
chase from Start to Grand Stand and Haven.

VI

The first morning of the meet arrived bright
and promising. The Grand Stand was filled
with a city crowd. The usual types of a race-
course appeared in force. Here and there
were to be seen the dog-grooms leading in
leash single Greyhounds or couples, shrouded
in blankets, but showing their sinewy legs, their
snaky necks, their shapely heads with long
reptilian jaws, and their quick, nervous yellow
eyes — hybrids of natural force and human

239

ingenuity, the most wonderful running-machines ever made of flesh and blood. Their keepers guarded them like jewels, tended them like babies, and were careful to keep them from picking up odd eatables, as well as prevent them smelling unusual objects or being approached by strangers. Large sums were wagered on these Dogs, and a cunningly placed tack, a piece of doctored meat, yes, an artfully compounded smell, has been known to turn a superb young runner into a lifeless laggard, and to the owner this might spell *ruin*. The Dogs entered in each class are paired off, as each contest is supposed to be a duel; the winners in the first series are then paired again. In each trial, a Jack is driven from the Starting-pen; close by in one leash are the rival Dogs, held by the slipper. As soon as the Hare is well away, the man has to get the Dogs evenly started and slip them together. On the field is the judge, scarlet-coated and well mounted. He follows the chase. The Hare, mindful of his training, speeds across the open, toward the Haven, in full view of the Grand Stand. The Dogs follow the Jack. As the first one

Little Warhorse

comes near enough to be dangerous, the Hare
balks him by dodging. Each time the Hare
is turned, scores for the Dog that did it, and a
final point is made by the kill.

Sometimes the kill takes place within one
hundred yards of the start—that means a poor
Jack; mostly it happens in front of the
Grand Stand; but on rare occasions it chances
that the Jack goes sailing across the open Park
a good half-mile and, by dodging for time, runs
to safety in the Haven. Four finishes are possible: a speedy kill; a speedy winning of the
Haven; new Dogs to relieve the first runners,
who would suffer heart-collapse in the terrific
strain of their pace, if kept up many minutes in
hot weather; and finally, for Rabbits that by
continued dodging defy and jeopardize the
Dogs, and yet do not win the Haven, there is
kept a *loaded shotgun.*

There is just as much jockeying at a Kaskado coursing as at a Kaskado horse-race,
just as many attempts at fraud, and it is just as
necessary to have the judge and slipper beyond
suspicion.

The day before the next meet a man of dia-

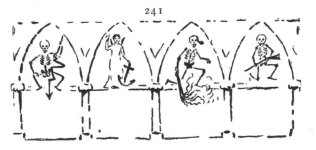

monds saw Irish Mickey—by chance. A cigar
was all that visibly passed, but it had a green
wrapper that was slipped off before lighting.
Then a word: "If you wuz slipper to-morrow
and it so came about that Dignam's Minkie gets
done, wall,—it means another cigar."

"Faix, an' if I wuz slipper I could load the
dice so Minkie would niver score a p'int, but her
runnin' mate would have the same bad luck."

"That so?" The diamond man looked interested. "All right—fix it so; it means two
cigars."

Slipper Slyman had always dealt on the
square, had scorned many approaches—that
was well known. Most believed in him, but
there were some malcontents, and when a man
with many gold seals approached the Steward
and formulated charges, serious and well-
backed, they must perforce suspend the slipper
pending an inquiry, and thus Mickey Doo
reigned in his stead.

Mickey was poor and not over-scrupulous.
Here was a chance to make a year's pay in a
minute, nothing wrong about it, no harm to the
Dog or the Rabbit either.

Little Warhorse

One Jack-rabbit is much like another. Everybody knows that; it was simply a question of choosing your Jack.

The preliminaries were over. Fifty Jacks had been run and killed. Mickey had done his work satisfactorily; a fair slip had been given to every leash. He was still in command as slipper. Now came the final for the cup—the cup and the large stakes.

VII

There were the slim and elegant Dogs awaiting their turn. Minkie and her rival were first. Everything had been fair so far, and who can say that what followed was unfair? Mickey could turn out which Jack he pleased.

"Number three!" he called to his partner.

Out leaped the Little Warhorse,—black and white his great ears, easy and low his five-foot bounds; gazing wildly at the unwonted crowd about the Park, he leaped high in one surprising spy-hop.

"Hrrrrr!" shouted the slipper, and his partner rattled a stick on the fence. The Warhorse's bounds increased to eight or nine feet.

Little Warhorse

" Hrrrrrr! " and they were ten or twelve feet. At thirty yards the Hounds were slipped—an even slip; some thought it could have been done at twenty yards.

" Hrrrrrr! Hrrrrrrr! " and the Warhorse was doing fourteen-foot leaps, not a spy-hop among them.

" Hrrrrr! " wonderful Dogs! how they sailed; but drifting ahead of them, like a white sea-bird or flying scud, was the Warhorse. Away past the Grand Stand. And the Dogs—were they closing the gap of start? Closing! It was lengthening! In less time than it takes to tell it, that black-and-white thistledown had drifted away through the Haven door,—the door so like that good old hen-hole,—and the Greyhounds pulled up amidst a roar of derision and cheers for the Little Warhorse. How Mickey did laugh! How Dignam did swear! How the newspaper men did scribble — scribble — scribble!

Next day there was a paragraph in all the papers: "WONDERFUL FEAT OF A JACKRABBIT. The Little Warhorse, as he has been styled, completely skunked two of the most famous Dogs on the turf," etc.

244

Little Warhorse

There was a fierce wrangle among the dog-men. This was a tie, since neither had scored, and Minkie and her rival were allowed to run again; but that half-mile had been too hot, and they had no show for the cup.

Mickey met "Diamonds" next day, *by chance.*

" Have a cigar, Mickey."

" Oi will thot, sor. Faix, thim 's so foine, I 'd loike two — thank ye, sor."

VIII

From that time the Little Warhorse became the pride of the Irish boy. Slipper Slyman had been honorably reinstated and Mickey reduced to the rank of Jack-starter, but that merely helped to turn his sympathies from the Dogs to the Rabbits, or rather to the Warhorse, for of all the five hundred that were brought in from the drive he alone had won renown. There were several that crossed the Park to run again another day, but he alone had crossed the course without getting even a turn. Twice a week the meets took place; forty or fifty Jacks were killed each time, and the five hundred in the pen had been nearly all eaten of the arena.

The Warhorse had run each day, and as often had made the Haven. Mickey became wildly enthusiastic about his favorite's powers. He begot a positive affection for the clean-limbed racer, and stoutly maintained against all that it was a positive honor to a Dog to be disgraced by such a Jack.

It is so seldom.that a Rabbit crosses the track at all, that when Jack did it six times without having to dodge, the papers took note of it, and after each meet there appeared a notice: "The Little Warhorse crossed again to-day; old-timers say it shows how our Dogs are deteriorating."

After the sixth time the rabbit-keepers grew enthusiastic, and Mickey, commander-in-chief of the brigade, became intemperate in his admiration. "Be jabers, he has a right to be torned loose. He has won his freedom loike ivery Amerikin done," he added, by way of appeal to the patriotism of the Steward of the race, who was, of course, the real owner of the Jacks.

Little Warhorse

"All right, Mick; if he gets across thirteen times you can ship him back to his native land," was the reply.

"Shure now, an' won't you make it tin, sor?"

"No, no; I need him to take the conceit out of some of the new Dogs that are coming."

"Thirteen toimes and he is free, sor; it's a bargain."

A new lot of Rabbits arrived about this time, and one of these was colored much like Little Warhorse. He had no such speed, but to prevent mistakes Mickey caught his favorite by driving him into one of the padded shipping-boxes, and proceeded with the gate-keeper's punch to earmark him. The punch was sharp; a clear star was cut out of the thin flap, when Mickey exclaimed: "Faix, an' Oi'll punch for ivery toime ye cross the coorse." So he cut six stars in a row. "Thayer now, Warrhorrse, shure it's a free Rabbit ye'll be when ye have yer thirteen stars loike our flag of liberty hed when *we* got free."

Within a week the Warhorse had vanquished the new Greyhounds and had stars enough to go round the right ear and begin on the left. In a week more the thirteen runs were completed, six stars in the left ear and seven in the right, and the newspapers had new material.

"Whoop!" How Mickey hoorayed! "An' it 's a free Jack ye are, Warrhorrse! Thirteen always wuz a lucky number. I never knowed it to fail."

IX

"Yes, I know I did," said the Steward. "But I want to give him one more run. I have a bet on him against a new Dog here. It won't hurt him now; he can do it. Oh, well. Here now, Mickey, don't you get sassy. One run more this afternoon. The Dogs run two or three times a day; why not the Jack?"

"They 're not shtakin' thayre loives, sor."

"Oh, you get out."

Many more Rabbits had been added to the pen,—big and small, peaceful and warlike,— and one big Buck of savage instincts, seeing Jack Warhorse's hurried dash into the Haven that morning, took advantage of the moment to attack him.

248

Little Warhorse

At another time Jack would have thumped
his skull, as he once did the Cat's, and settled
the affair in a minute; but now it took several
minutes, during which he himself got roughly
handled; so when the afternoon came he was
suffering from one or two bruises and stiffening
wounds; not serious, indeed, but enough to
lower his speed.

The start was much like those of previous
runs. The Warhorse steaming away low and
lightly, his ears up and the breezes whistling
through his thirteen stars.

Minkie with Fango, the new Dog, bounded
in eager pursuit, but, to the surprise of the
starters, the gap grew smaller. The Warhorse
was losing ground, and right before the Grand
Stand old Minkie turned him, and a cheer
went up from the dog-men, for all knew the
runners. Within fifty yards Fango scored a
turn, and the race was right back to the start.
There stood Slyman and Mickey. The Rabbit dodged, the Greyhounds plunged; Jack
could not get away, and just as the final snap
seemed near, the Warhorse leaped straight
for Mickey, and in an instant was hidden in his

arms, while the starter's feet flew out in energetic kicks to repel the furious Dogs. It is not likely that the Jack knew Mickey for a friend; he only yielded to the old instinct to fly from a certain enemy to a neutral or a possible friend, and, as luck would have it, he had wisely leaped and well. A cheer went up from the benches as Mickey hurried back with his favorite. But the dog-men protested "it was n't a fair run—they wanted it finished." They appealed to the Steward. He had backed the Jack against Fango. He was sore now, and ordered a new race.

An hour's rest was the best Mickey could get for him. Then he went as before, with Fango and Minkie in pursuit. He seemed less stiff now—he ran more like himself; but a little past the Stand he was turned by Fango and again by Minkie, and back and across, and here and there, leaping frantically and barely eluding his foes. For several minutes it lasted. Mickey could see that Jack's ears were sinking. The new Dog leaped. Jack dodged almost under him to escape, and back only to meet the second Dog; and now both ears were flat on his back. But

Little Warhorse

the Hounds were suffering too. Their tongues
were lolling out; their jaws and heaving sides
were splashed with foam. The Warhorse's ears
went up again. His courage seemed to revive
in their distress. He made a straight dash for
the Haven; but the straight dash was just what
the Hounds could do, and within a hundred
yards he was turned again, to begin another
desperate game of zigzag. Then the dog-men
saw danger for their Dogs, and two new ones
were slipped—two fresh Hounds; surely they
could end the race. *But they did not.* The
first two were vanquished—gasping—out of it,
but the next two were racing near. The Warhorse put forth all his strength. He left the
first two far behind — was nearly to the Haven
when the second two came up.

Nothing but dodging could save him now.
His ears were sinking, his heart was patter-
ing on his ribs, but his spirit was strong.
He flung himself in wildest zigzags. The
Hounds tumbled over each other. Again and
again they thought they had him. One of
them snapped off the end of his long black tail,
yet he escaped; but he could not get to the

Little Warhorse

Haven. The luck was against him. He was
forced nearer to the Grand Stand. A thousand
ladies were watching. The time limit was up.
The second Dogs were suffering, when Mickey
came running, yelling like a madman—words
—imprecations—crazy sounds:

"Ye blackguard hoodlums! Ye dhirty, cow-
ardly bastes!" and he rushed furiously at the
Dogs, intent to do them bodily harm.

Officers came running and shouting, and
Mickey, shrieking hatred and defiance, was
dragged from the field, reviling Dogs and men
with every horrid, insulting name he could think
of or invent.

"Fair play! Whayer's yer fair play, ye liars,
ye dhirty cheats, ye bloody cowards!" And
they drove him from the arena. The last he saw
of it was the four foaming Dogs feebly dodging
after a weak and worn-out Jack-rabbit, and the
judge on his Horse beckoning to the man with
the gun.

The gate closed behind him, and Mickey
heard a *bang — bang*, an unusual uproar mixed
with yelps of Dogs, and he knew that Little Jack
Warhorse had been served with finish No. 4.

The second Dogs were suffering.

Little Warhorse

All his life he had loved Dogs, but his sense
of fair play was outraged. He could not get
in, nor see in from where he was. He raced
along the lane to the Haven, where he might
get a good view, and arrived in time to see —
Little Jack Warhorse with his half-masted ears
limp into the Haven; and he realized at once
that the man with the gun had missed, had hit
the wrong runner, for there was the crowd at
the Stand watching two men who were carrying
a wounded Greyhound, while a veterinary sur-
geon was ministering to another that was panting on the ground.

Mickey looked about, seized a little shipping-
box, put it at the angle of the Haven, carefully
drove the tired thing into it, closed the lid,
then, with the box under his arm, he scaled the
fence unseen in the confusion and was gone.

'It did n't matter; he had lost his job anyway.' He tramped away from the city. He
took the train at the nearest station and travelled some hours, and now he was in Rabbit
country again. The sun had long gone down;
the night with its stars was over the plain when
among the farms, the Osage and alfalfa, Mickey

Little Warhorse

Doo opened the box and gently put the War-horse out.

Grinning as he did so, he said: "Shure an' it 's ould Oireland thot 's proud to set the thirteen stars at liberty wance moore."

For a moment the Little Warhorse gazed in doubt, then took three or four long leaps and a spy-hop to get his bearings. Now spreading his national colors and his honor-marked ears, he bounded into his hard-won freedom, strong as ever, and melted into the night of his native plain.

He has been seen many times in Kaskado, and there have been many Rabbit drives in that region, but he seems to know some means of baffling them now, for, in all the thousands that have been trapped and corralled, they have never since seen the star-spangled ears of Little Jack Warhorse.

256

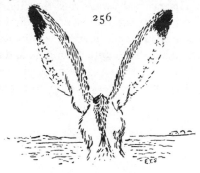

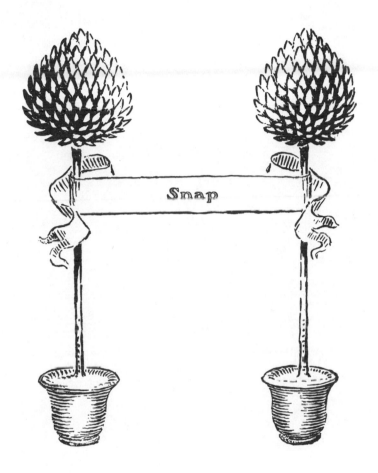

Snap

The Story of a Bull-terrier

I

T was dusk on Hallowe'en when first I saw him. Early in the morning I had received a telegram from my college chum Jack: "Lest we forget. Am sending you a remarkable pup. Be polite to him; it 's safer." It would have been just like Jack to have sent an infernal machine or a Skunk rampant and called it a pup, so I awaited the hamper with curiosity. When it arrived I saw it was marked "Dangerous," and there came from within a high-pitched snarl at every

259

slight provocation.　On peering through the wire netting I saw it was not a baby Tiger but a small white Bull-terrier.　He snapped at me and at any one or anything that seemed too abrupt or too near for proper respect, and his snarling growl was unpleasantly frequent.　Dogs have two growls: one deep-rumbled, and chesty; that is polite warning—the retort courteous; the other mouthy and much higher in pitch: this is the last word before actual onslaught. The Terrier's growls were all of the latter kind. I was a dog-man and thought I knew all about Dogs, so, dismissing the porter, I got out my all-round jackknife - toothpick - nailhammer-hatch-et-toolbox-fire-shovel, a specialty of our firm, and lifted the netting.　Oh, yes, I knew all about Dogs.　The little fury had been growling out a whole-souled growl for every tap of the tool, and when I turned the box on its side, he made a dash straight for my legs.　Had not his foot gone through the wire netting and held him, I might have been hurt, for his heart was evidently in his work; but I stepped on the table out of reach and tried to reason with him.　I have always believed in talking to animals.　I

Snap

maintain that they gather something of our intention at least, even if they do not understand our words; but the Dog evidently put me down for a hypocrite and scorned my approaches. At first he took his post under the table and kept up a circular watch for a leg trying to get down. I felt sure I could have controlled him with my eye, but I could not bring it to bear where I was, or rather where he was; thus I was left a prisoner. I am a very cool person, I flatter myself; in fact, I represent a hardware firm, and, in coolness, we are not excelled by any but perhaps the nosy gentlemen that sell wearing-apparel. I got out a cigar and smoked tailor-style on the table, while my little tyrant below kept watch for legs. I got out the telegram and read it: "Remarkable pup. Be polite to him; it's safer." I think it was my coolness rather than my politeness that did it, for in half an hour the growling ceased. In an hour he no longer jumped at a newspaper cautiously pushed over the edge to test his humor; possibly the irritation of the cage was wearing off, and by the time I had lit my third cigar, he waddled out to the fire and lay down; not ignoring me,

however, I had no reason to complain of that
kind of contempt. He kept one eye on me,
and I kept both eyes, not on him, but on his
stumpy tail. If that tail should swing sidewise
once I should feel I was winning; but it did
not swing. I got a book and put in time on
that table till my legs were cramped and the
fire burned low. About 10 P.M. it was chilly,
and at half-past ten the fire was out. My
Hallowe'en present got up, yawned and
stretched, then walked under my bed, where he
found a fur rug. By stepping lightly from the
table to the dresser, and then on to the mantel-
shelf, I also reached bed, and, very quietly un-
dressing, got in without provoking any criticism
from my master. I had not yet fallen asleep
when I heard a slight scrambling and felt
"thump-thump" on the bed, then over my feet
and legs; Snap evidently had found it too cool
down below, and proposed to have the best
my house afforded.

He curled up on my feet in such a way that
I was very uncomfortable and tried to readjust
matters, but the slightest wriggle of my toe was
enough to make him snap at it so fiercely that

Snap

nothing but thick woollen bedclothes saved me from being maimed for life.

I was an hour moving my feet—a hair's-breadth at a time—till they were so that I could sleep in comfort; and I was awakened several times during the night by angry snarls from the Dog—I suppose because I dared to move a toe without his approval, though once I believe he did it simply because I was snoring.

In the morning I was ready to get up before Snap was. You see, I call him Snap—Ginger-snap in full. Some Dogs are hard to name, and some do not seem to need it—they name themselves.

I was ready to rise at seven. Snap was not ready till eight, so we rose at eight. He had little to say to the man who made the fire. He allowed me to dress without doing it on the table. As I left the room to get breakfast, I remarked:

"Snap, my friend, some men would whip you into a different way, but I think I know a better plan. The doctors nowadays favor the 'no-breakfast cure.' I shall try that."

It seemed cruel, but I left him without food

To Doctor
G. Richquick's
SANITARIUM

all day. It cost me something to repaint the door where he scratched it, but at night he was quite ready to accept a little food at my hands.

In a week we were very good friends. He would sleep on my bed now and allow me to move my feet without snapping at them, intent to do me serious bodily harm. The no-breakfast cure had worked wonders; in three months we were—well, simply man and Dog, and he amply justified the telegram he came with.

He seemed to be without fear. If a small Dog came near, he would take not the slightest notice; if a medium-sized Dog, he would stick his stub of a tail rigidly up in the air, then walk around him, scratching contemptuously with his hind feet, and looking at the sky, the distance, the ground, anything but the Dog, and noting his presence only by frequent high-pitched growls. If the stranger did not move on at once, the battle began, and then the stranger usually moved on very rapidly. Snap sometimes got worsted, but no amount of sad experience could ever inspire him with a grain of caution. Once, while riding in a cab

Snap.

Snap

during the Dog Show, Snap caught sight of an elephantine St. Bernard taking an airing. Its size aroused such enthusiasm in the Pup's little breast that he leaped from the cab window to do battle, and broke his leg.

Evidently fear had been left out of his make-up and its place supplied with an extra amount of ginger, which was the reason of his full name. He differed from all other Dogs I have ever known. For example, if a boy threw a stone at him, he ran, not away, but toward the boy, and if the crime was repeated, Snap took the law into his own hands; thus he was at least respected by all. Only myself and the porter at the office seemed to realize his good points, and we only were admitted to the high honor of personal friendship, an honor which I appreciated more as months went on, and by midsummer not Carnegie, Vanderbilt, and Astor together could have raised money enough to buy a quarter of a share in my little Dog Snap.

Snap

II

Though not a regular traveller, I was ordered out on the road in the autumn, and then Snap and the landlady were left together, with unfortunate developments. Contempt on his part—fear on hers; and hate on both.

I was placing a lot of barb-wire in the northern tier of States. My letters were forwarded once a week, and I got several complaints from the landlady about Snap.

Arrived at Mendoza, in North Dakota, I found a fine market for wire. Of course my dealings were with the big storekeepers, but I went about among the ranchmen to get their practical views on the different styles, and thus I met the Penroof Brothers' Cow-outfit.

One cannot be long in Cow country now without hearing a great deal about the depredations of the ever wily and destructive Gray-wolf. The day has gone by when they can be poisoned wholesale, and they are a serious drain on the rancher's profits. The Penroof Brothers, like most live cattle-men, had given

Snap

up all attempts at poisoning and trapping, and
were trying various breeds of Dogs as Wolf-
hunters, hoping to get a little sport out of the
necessary work of destroying the pests.

Foxhounds had failed—they were too soft
for fighting; Great Danes were too clumsy,
and Greyhounds could not follow the game
unless they could see it.   Each breed had
some fatal defect, but the cow-men hoped to
succeed with a mixed pack, and the day when
I was invited to join in a Mendoza Wolf-hunt,
I was amused by the variety of Dogs that
followed.   There were several mongrels, but
there were also a few highly bred Dogs—in
particular, some Russian Wolfhounds that must
have cost a lot of money.

Hilton Penroof, the oldest boy, "The Master
of Hounds," was unusually proud of them, and
expected them to do great things.

"Greyhounds are too thin-skinned to fight
a Wolf, Danes are too slow, but you 'll see the
fur fly when the Russians take a hand."

Thus the Greyhounds were there as runners,
the Danes as heavy backers, and the Russians
to do the important fighting.   There were also

two or three Foxhounds, whose fine noses were relied on to follow the trail if the game got out of view.

It was a fine sight as we rode away among the Badland Buttes that October day. The air was bright and crisp, and though so late, there was neither snow nor frost. The Horses were fresh, and once or twice showed me how a Cow-pony tries to get rid of his rider.

The Dogs were keen for sport, and we did start one or two gray spots in the plain that Hilton said were Wolves or Coyotes. The Dogs trailed away at full cry, but at night, beyond the fact that one of the Greyhounds had a wound on his shoulder, there was nothing to show that any of them had been on a Wolf-hunt.

"It 's my opinion yer fancy Russians is no good, Hilt," said Garvin, the younger brother. "I 'll back that little black Dane against the lot, mongrel an' all as he is."

"I don't unnerstan' it," growled Hilton. "There ain't a Coyote, let alone a Gray-wolf, kin run away from them Greyhounds; them Foxhounds kin folly a trail three days old, an' the Danes could lick a Grizzly."

Snap

"I reckon," said the father, "they kin run, an' they kin track, an' they kin lick a Grizzly, *maybe*, but the fac' is they don't want to tackle a Gray-wolf. The hull darn pack is scairt— an' I wish we had our money out o' them."

Thus the men grumbled and discussed as I drove away and left them.

There seemed only one solution of the failure. The Hounds were swift and strong, but a Gray-wolf seems to terrorize all Dogs. They have not the nerve to face him, and so, each time he gets away, and my thoughts flew back to the fearless little Dog that had shared my bed for the last year. How I wished he was out here, then these lubberly giants of Hounds would find a leader whose nerve would not fail at the moment of trial.

At Baroka, my next stop, I got a batch of mail including two letters from the landlady; the first to say that "that beast of a Dog was acting up scandalous in my room," and the other still more forcible, demanding his immediate removal.

"Why not have him expressed to Mendoza?" I thought. "It's only twenty hours; they'll

be glad to have him.   I can take him home
with me when I go through."

III

My next meeting with Gingersnap was not
as different from the first as one might have expected.   He jumped on me, made much vig-
orous pretense to bite, and growled frequently,
but it was a deep-chested growl and his stump
waggled hard.

The Penroofs had had a number of Wolf-
hunts since I was with them, and were much
disgusted at having no better success than before.   The Dogs could find a Wolf nearly every
time they went out, but they could not kill him,
and the men were not near enough at the finish
to learn why.

Old Penroof was satisfied that "thar was n't
one of the hull miserable gang that had the
grit of a Jack-rabbit."

We were off at dawn the next day—the
same procession of fine Horses and superb
riders; the big blue Dogs, the yellow Dogs, the
spotted Dogs, as before; but there was a new

272

Snap

feature, a little white Dog that stayed close by
me, and not only any Dogs, but Horses that
came too near were apt to get a surprise from
his teeth. I think he quarrelled with every
man, Horse, and Dog in the country, with the
exception of a Bull-terrier belonging to the
Mendoza hotel man. She was the only one
smaller than himself, and they seemed very
good friends.

I shall never forget the view of the hunt I
had that day. We were on one of those large,
flat-headed buttes that give a kingdom to the
eye, when Hilton, who had been scanning the
vast country with glasses, exclaimed: "I see
him. There he goes, toward Skull Creek.
Guess it 's a Coyote."

Now the first thing is to get the Greyhounds
to see the prey—not an easy matter, as they cannot use the glasses, and the ground was covered
with sage-brush higher than the Dogs' heads.

But Hilton called, " Hu, hu, Dander," and
leaned aside from his saddle, holding out his
foot at the same time. With one agile bound
Dander leaped to the saddle and there stood
balancing on the Horse while Hilton kept point-

ing. "There he is, Dander; sic him — see him down there." The Dog gazed earnestly where his master pointed, then seeming to see, he sprang to the ground with a slight yelp and sped away. The other Dogs followed after, in an ever-lengthening procession, and we rode as hard as we could behind them, but losing time, for the ground was cut with gullies, spotted with badger-holes, and covered with rocks and sage that made full speed too hazardous.

We all fell behind, and I was last, of course, being least accustomed to the saddle. We got several glimpses of the Dogs flying over the level plain or dropping from sight in gullies to reappear at the other side. Dander, the Greyhound, was the recognized leader, and as we mounted another ridge we got sight of the whole chase — a Coyote at full speed, the Dogs a quarter of a mile behind, but gaining. When next we saw them the Coyote was dead, and the Dogs sitting around panting, all but two of the Foxhounds and Gingersnap.

"Too late for the fracas," remarked Hilton, glancing at these last Foxhounds. Then he

Snap

proudly petted Dander. " Did n't need yer
purp after all, ye see."

" Takes a heap of nerve for ten big Dogs to
face one little Coyote," remarked the father,
sarcastically. " Wait till we run onto a Gray."

Next day we were out again, for I made up
my mind to see it to a finish.

From a high point we caught sight of a
moving speck of gray. A moving white speck
stands for Antelope, a red speck for Fox, a
gray speck for either Gray-wolf or Coyote, and
which of these is determined by its tail. If the
glass shows the tail down, it is a Coyote; if up,
it is the hated Gray-wolf.

Dander was shown the game as before and
led the motley mixed procession—as he had
before—Greyhounds, Wolfhounds, Foxhounds,
Danes, Bull-terrier, horsemen. We got a momentary view of the pursuit; a Gray-wolf it
surely was, loping away ahead of the Dogs.
Somehow I thought the first Dogs were not
running so fast now as they had after the Coyote. But no one knew the finish of the hunt.
The Dogs came back to us one by one, and we
saw no more of that Wolf.

Snap

Sarcastic remarks and recrimination were now freely indulged in by the hunters.

"Pah! scairt, plumb scairt," was the father's disgusted comment on the pack. "They could catch up easy enough, but when he turned on them, they lighted out for home—pah!"

"Where 's that thar onsurpassable, fearless, scaired-o'-nort Tarrier?" asked Hilton, scornfully.

"I don't know," said I. "I am inclined to think he never saw the Wolf; but if he ever does, I 'll bet he sails in for death or glory."

That night several Cows were killed close to the ranch, and we were spurred on to another hunt.

It opened much like the last. Late in the afternoon we sighted a gray fellow with tail up, not half a mile off. Hilton called Dander up on the saddle. I acted on the idea and called Snap to mine. His legs were so short that he had to leap several times before he made it, scrambling up at last with my foot as a half-way station. I pointed and "sic-ed" for a minute before he saw the game, and then he started out after the Greyhounds, already gone, with energy that was full of promise.

Snap

The chase this time led us, not to the rough brakes along the river, but toward the high open country, for reasons that appeared later. We were close together as we rose to the upland and sighted the chase half a mile off, just as Dander came up with the Wolf and snapped at his haunch. The Gray-wolf turned round to fight, and we had a fine view. The Dogs came up by twos and threes, barking at him in a ring, till last the little white one rushed up. He wasted no time barking, but rushed straight at the Wolf's throat and missed it, yet seemed to get him by the nose; then the ten big Dogs closed in, and in two minutes the Wolf was dead. We had ridden hard to be in at the finish, and though our view was distant, we saw at least that Snap had lived up to the telegram, as well as to my promises for him.

Now it was my turn to crow, and I did not lose the chance. Snap had shown them how, and at last the Mendoza pack had killed a Gray-wolf without help from the men.

There were two things to mar the victory somewhat: first, it was a young Wolf, a mere

Snap

Cub, hence his foolish choice of country; second, Snap was wounded—the Wolf had given him a bad cut in the shoulder.

As we rode in proud procession home, I saw he limped a little. "Here," I cried, "come up, Snap." He tried once or twice to jump to the saddle, but could not. "Here, Hilton, lift him up to me."

"Thanks; I 'll let you handle your own rattlesnakes," was the reply, for all knew now that it was not safe to meddle with his person. "Here, Snap, take hold," I said, and held my quirt to him. He seized it, and by that I lifted him to the front of my saddle and so carried him home. I cared for him as though he had been a baby. He had shown those Cattle-men how to fill the weak place in their pack; the Foxhounds may be good and the Greyhounds swift and the Russians and Danes fighters, but they are no use at all without the crowning moral force of grit, that none can supply so well as a Bull-terrier. On that day the Cattle-men learned how to manage the Wolf question, as you will find if ever you are at Mendoza; for every successful Wolf pack there has with

Snap

it a Bull-terrier, preferably of the Snap-Mendoza
breed.

IV

Next day was Hallowe'en, the anniversary
of Snap's advent. The weather was clear,
bright, not too cold, and there was no snow on
the ground. The men usually celebrated the
day with a hunt of some sort, and now, of
course, Wolves were the one object. To the
disappointment of all, Snap was in bad shape
with his wound. He slept, as usual, at my feet,
and bloody stains now marked the place. He
was not in condition to fight, but we were
bound to have a Wolf-hunt, so he was beguiled
to an outhouse and locked up, while we went
off, I, at least, with a sense of impending disaster. I *knew* we should fail without my Dog,
but I did not realize how bad a failure it was
to be.

Afar among the buttes of Skull Creek we had
roamed when a white ball appeared bounding
through the sage-brush, and in a minute more
Snap came, growling and stump-waggling, up
to my Horse's side. I could not send him back;

Snap

he would take no such orders, not even from me. His wound was looking bad, so I called him, held down the quirt, and jumped him to my saddle.

"There," I thought, "I 'll keep you safe till we get home." Yes, I thought; but I reckoned not with Snap. The voice of Hilton, "Hu, hu," announced that he had sighted a Wolf. Dander and Riley, his rival, both sprang to the point of observation, with the result that they collided and fell together, sprawling, in the sage. But Snap, gazing hard, had sighted the Wolf, not so very far off, and before I knew it, he leaped from the saddle and bounded zigzag, high, low, in and under the sage, straight for the enemy, leading the whole pack for a few minutes. Not far, of course. The great Greyhounds sighted the moving speck, and the usual procession strung out on the plain. It promised to be a fine hunt, for the Wolf had less than half a mile start and all the Dogs were fully interested.

"They 've turned up Grizzly Gully," cried Garvin. "This way, and we can head them off."

Snap

So we turned and rode hard around the
north side of Hulmer's Butte, while the chase
seemed to go round the south.

We galloped to the top of Cedar Ridge and
were about to ride down, when Hilton shouted,
" By George, here he is! We 're right onto
him." He leaped from his Horse, dropped the
bridle, and ran forward. I did the same. A
great Gray-wolf came lumbering across an
open plain toward us. His head was low, his
tail out level, and fifty yards behind him was
Dander, sailing like a Hawk over the ground,
going twice as fast as the Wolf. In a minute
the Hound was alongside and snapped, but
bounded back, as the Wolf turned on him. They
were just below us now and not fifty feet away.
Garvin drew his revolver, but in a fateful moment Hilton interfered : " No ; no ; let 's see it
out." In a few seconds the next Greyhound
arrived, then the rest in order of swiftness.
Each came up full of fight and fury, determined
to go right in and tear the Gray-wolf to pieces ;
but each in turn swerved aside, and leaped and
barked around at a safe distance. After a
minute or so the Russians appeared—fine big

Snap

Dogs they were. Their distant intention no doubt was to dash right at the old Wolf; but his fearless front, his sinewy frame and death-dealing jaws, awed them long before they were near him, and they also joined the ring, while the desperado in the middle faced this way and that, ready for any or all.

Now the Danes came up, huge-limbed creatures, any one of them as heavy as the Wolf. I heard their heavy breathing tighten into a threatening sound as they plunged ahead, eager to tear the foe to pieces; but when they saw him there, grim, fearless, mighty of jaw, tireless of limb, ready to die if need be, but sure of this, he would not die alone—well, those great Danes—all three of them—were stricken, as the rest had been, with a sudden bashfulness: yes, they would go right in presently—not now, but as soon as they had got their breath; they were not afraid of a Wolf, oh, no. I could read their courage in their voices. They knew perfectly well that the first Dog to go in was going to get hurt, but never mind that—presently; they would bark a little more to get up enthusiasm.

The bounding ball of white.

Snap

And as the ten big Dogs were leaping round the silent Wolf at bay, there was a rustling in the sage at the far side of the place; then a snow-white rubber ball, it seemed, came bounding, but grew into a little Bull-terrier, and Snap, slowest of the pack, and last, came panting hard, so hard he seemed gasping. Over the level open he made, straight to the changing ring around the Cattle-killer whom none dared face. Did he hesitate? Not for an instant; through the ring of the yelping pack, straight for the old despot of the range, right for his throat, he sprang; and the Gray-wolf struck with his twenty scimitars. But the little one, if foiled at all, sprang again, and then what came I hardly knew. There was a whirling mass of Dogs. I thought I saw the little White One clinched on the Gray-wolf's nose. The pack was all around; we could not help them now. But they did not need us; they had a leader of dauntless mettle, and when in a little while the final scene was done, there on the ground lay the Gray-wolf, a giant of his kind, and clinched on his nose was the little white Dog.

We were standing around within fifteen feet,

Snap

ready to help, but had no chance till we were
not needed.

The Wolf was dead, and I hallooed to Snap,
but he did not move. I bent over him. "Snap
—Snap, it 's all over; you 've killed him." But
the Dog was very still, and now I saw two
deep wounds in his body. I tried to lift him.
" Let go, old fellow; it 's all over." He growled
feebly, and at last let go of the Wolf. The
rough cattle-men were kneeling around him
now; old Penroof's voice was trembling as he
muttered, " I would n't had him hurt for twenty
steers." I lifted him in my arms, called to him
and stroked his head. He snarled a little, a
farewell as it proved, for he licked my hand as
he did so, then never snarled again.

That was a sad ride home for me. There
was the skin of a monstrous Wolf, but no other
hint of triumph. We buried the fearless one
on a butte back of the ranch-house. Penroof, as he stood by, was heard to grumble:
" By jingo, that was grit—cl'ar grit! Ye can't
raise Cattle without grit."

286

The Winnipeg Wolf

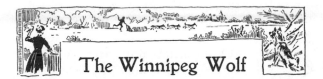

The Winnipeg Wolf

I

T was during the great blizzard of 1882 that I first met the Winnipeg Wolf. I had left St. Paul in the middle of March to cross the prairies to Winnipeg, expecting to be there in twenty-four hours, but the Storm King had planned it otherwise and sent a heavy-laden eastern blast. The snow came down in a furious, steady torrent, hour after hour. Never before had I seen such a storm. All the world was lost in snow —snow, snow, snow—whirling, biting, stinging, drifting snow—and the puffing, monstrous engine was compelled to stop at the command of those tiny, feathery crystals of spotless purity.

The Winnipeg Wolf

Many strong hands with shovels came to the delicately curled snowdrifts that barred our way, and in an hour the engine could pass—only to stick in another drift yet farther on. It was dreary work—day after day, night after night, sticking in the drifts, digging ourselves out, and still the snow went whirling and playing about us.

"Twenty-two hours to Emerson," said the official; but nearly two weeks of digging passed before we did reach Emerson, and the poplar country where the thickets stop all drifting of the snow. Thenceforth the train went swiftly, the poplar woods grew more thickly—we passed for miles through solid forests, then perhaps through an open space. As we neared St. Boniface, the eastern outskirts of Winnipeg, we dashed across a little glade fifty yards wide, and there in the middle was a group that stirred me to the very soul.

In plain view was a great rabble of Dogs, large and small, black, white, and yellow, wriggling and heaving this way and that way in a rude ring; to one side was a little yellow Dog stretched and quiet in the snow; on the outer

The Winnipeg Wolf

part of the ring was a huge black Dog bounding about and barking, but keeping ever behind the moving mob. And in the midst, the centre and cause of it all, was a great, grim, Wolf.

Wolf? He looked like a Lion. There he stood, all alone—resolute—calm—with bristling mane, and legs braced firmly, glancing this way and that, to be ready for an attack in any direction. There was a curl on his lips—it looked like scorn, but I suppose it was really the fighting snarl of tooth display. Led by a wolfish-looking Dog that should have been ashamed, the pack dashed in, for the twentieth time no doubt. But the great gray form leaped here and there, and chop, chop, chop went those fearful jaws, no other sound from the lonely warrior; but a death yelp from more than one of his foes, as those that were able again sprang back, and left him statuesque as before, untamed, unmaimed, and contemptuous of them all.

How I wished for the train to stick in a snowdrift now, as so often before, for all my heart went out to that Gray-wolf; I longed to go and help him. But the snow-deep glade flashed by, the poplar trunks shut out the view, and we went on to our journey's end.

This was all I saw, and it seemed little; but before many days had passed I knew surely that I had been favored with a view, in broad daylight, of a rare and wonderful creature, none less than the Winnipeg Wolf.

His was a strange history—a Wolf that preferred the city to the country, that passed by the Sheep to kill the Dogs, and that always hunted alone.

In telling the story of *le Garou*, as he was called by some, although I speak of these things as locally familiar, it is very sure that to many citizens of the town they were quite unknown. The smug shopkeeper on the main street had scarcely heard of him until the day after the final scene at the slaughter-house, when his great carcass was carried to Hine's taxidermist shop and there mounted, to be exhibited later at the Chicago World's Fair, and to be destroyed, alas! in the fire that reduced the Mulvey Grammar School to ashes in 1896.

Surrounded by a score of Dogs was a Great Gray-wolf.

The Winnipeg Wolf

II

It seems that Fiddler Paul, the handsome ne'er-do-well of the half-breed world, readier to hunt than to work, was prowling with his gun along the wooded banks of the Red River by Kildonan, one day in the June of 1880. He saw a Gray-wolf come out of a hole in a bank and fired a chance shot that killed it. Having made sure, by sending in his Dog, that no other large Wolf was there, he crawled into the den, and found, to his utter amazement and delight, eight young Wolves—nine bounties of ten dollars each. How much is that? A fortune surely. He used a stick vigorously, and with the assistance of the yellow Cur, all the little ones were killed but one. There is a superstition about the last of a brood—it is not lucky to kill it. So Paul set out for town with the scalp of the old Wolf, the scalps of the seven young, and the last Cub alive.

The saloon-keeper, who got the dollars for which the scalps were exchanged, soon got the living Cub. He grew up at the end of a chain, but developed a chest and jaws that no Hound

in town could match. He was kept in the
yard for the amusement of customers, and this
amusement usually took the form of baiting
the captive with Dogs. The young Wolf was
bitten and mauled nearly to death on several
occasions, but he recovered, and each month
there were fewer Dogs willing to face him.
His life was as hard as it could be. There
was but one gleam of gentleness in it all, and
that was the friendship that grew up between
himself and Little Jim, the son of the saloon-
keeper.

Jim was a wilful little rascal with a mind of
his own. He took to the Wolf because it had
killed a Dog that had bitten him. He thenceforth fed the Wolf and made a pet of it, and
the Wolf responded by allowing him to take
liberties which no one else dared venture.

Jim's father was not a model parent. He
usually spoiled his son, but at times would get
in a rage and beat him cruelly for some trifle.
The child was quick to learn that he was beaten,
not because he had done wrong, but because he
had made his father angry. If, therefore, he
could keep out of the way until that anger had

The Winnipeg Wolf

cooled, he had no further cause for worry. One day, seeking safety in flight with his father behind him, he dashed into the Wolf's kennel, and his grizzly chum thus unceremoniously awakened turned to the door, displayed a double row of ivories, and plainly said to the father: "Don't you dare to touch him."

If Hogan could have shot the Wolf then and there he would have done so, but the chances were about equal of killing his son, so he let them alone and, half an hour later, laughed at the whole affair. Thenceforth Little Jim made for the Wolf's den whenever he was in danger, and sometimes the only notice any one had that the boy had been in mischief was seeing him sneak in behind the savage captive.

Economy in hired help was a first principle with Hogan. Therefore his "barkeep" was a Chinaman. He was a timid, harmless creature, so Paul des Roches did not hesitate to bully him. One day, finding Hogan out, and the Chinaman alone in charge, Paul, already tipsy, demanded a drink on credit, and Tung Ling, acting on standing orders, refused. His artless

explanation, "No good, neber pay," so far from clearing up the difficulty, brought Paul staggering back of the bar to avenge the insult. The Celestial might have suffered grievous bodily hurt, but that Little Jim was at hand and had a long stick, with which he adroitly tripped up the Fiddler and sent him sprawling. He staggered to his feet swearing he would have Jim's life. But the child was near the back door and soon found refuge in the Wolf's kennel.

Seeing that the boy had a protector, Paul got the long stick, and from a safe distance began to belabor the Wolf. The grizzly creature raged at the end of the chain, but, though he parried many cruel blows by seizing the stick in his teeth, he was suffering severely, when Paul realized that Jim, whose tongue had not been idle, was fumbling away with nervous fingers to set the Wolf loose, and soon would succeed. Indeed, it would have been done already but for the strain that the Wolf kept on the chain.

The thought of being in the yard at the mercy of the huge animal that he had so enraged, gave the brave Paul a thrill of terror.

The Winnipeg Wolf

Jim's wheedling voice was heard—"Hold on now, Wolfie; back up just a little, and you shall have him. Now do; there 's a good Wolfie"—that was enough; the Fiddler fled and carefully closed all doors behind him.

Thus the friendship between Jim and his pet grew stronger, and the Wolf, as he developed his splendid natural powers, gave daily evidence also of the mortal hatred he bore to men that smelt of whiskey and to all Dogs, the causes of his sufferings. This peculiarity, coupled with his love for the child—and all children seemed to be included to some extent—grew with his growth and seemed to prove the ruling force of his life.

III

At this time—that is, the fall of 1881—there were great complaints among the Qu'Appelle ranchmen that the Wolves were increasing in their country and committing great depredations among the stock. Poisoning and trapping had proved failures, and when a distinguished German visitor appeared at the Club in Winnipeg and announced that he was bringing some Dogs that could easily rid the country of Wolves, he was listened to with unusual interest. For the cattle-men are fond of sport, and the idea of helping their business by establishing a kennel of Wolfhounds was very alluring.

The German soon produced as samples of his Dogs, two magnificent Danes, one white, the other blue with black spots and a singular white eye that completed an expression of unusual ferocity. Each of these great creatures weighed nearly two hundred pounds. They were muscled like Tigers, and the German was readily believed when he claimed that these two alone were more than a match for the biggest Wolf. He thus described their method of hunting: "All you have to do is show them the trail and, even if it is a day old, away they go on it. They cannot be shaken off. They will soon find that Wolf, no matter how he doubles and hides. Then they close on him. He turns to run, the blue Dog takes him by the haunch and throws him like this," and the German jerked a roll of bread into the air; "then before he touches the ground the white

The Winnipeg Wolf

Dog has his head, the other his tail, and they pull him apart like that."

It sounded all right; at any rate every one was eager to put it to the proof. Several of the residents said there was a fair chance of finding a Gray-wolf along the Assiniboine, so a hunt was organized. But they searched in vain for three days and were giving it up when some one suggested that down at Hogan's saloon was a Wolf chained up, that they could get for the value of the bounty, and though little more than a year old he would serve to show what the Dogs could do.

The value of Hogan's Wolf went up at once when he knew the importance of the occasion; besides, "he had conscientious scruples." All his scruples vanished, however, when his views as to price were met. His first care was to get Little Jim out of the way by sending him on an errand to his grandma's; then the Wolf was driven into his box and nailed in. The box was put in a wagon and taken to the open prairie along the Portage trail.

The Dogs could scarcely be held back, they were so eager for the fray, as soon as they smelt the Wolf. But several strong men held their leash, the wagon was drawn half a mile farther, and the Wolf was turned out with some difficulty. At first he looked scared and sullen. He tried to get out of sight, but made no attempt to bite. However, on finding himself free, as well as hissed and hooted at, he started off at a slinking trot toward the south, where the land seemed broken. The Dogs were released at that moment, and, baying furiously, they bounded away after the young Wolf. The men cheered loudly and rode behind them. From the very first it was clear that he had no chance. The Dogs were much swifter; the white one could run like a Greyhound. The German was wildly enthusiastic as she flew across the prairie, gaining visibly on the Wolf at every second. Many bets were offered on the Dogs, but there were no takers. The only bets accepted were Dog against Dog. The young Wolf went at speed now, but within a mile the white Dog was right behind him—was closing in.

The German shouted: " Now watch and see that Wolf go up in the air."

The Winnipeg Wolf

In a moment the runners were together.
Both recoiled, neither went up in the air, but
the white Dog rolled over with a fearful gash
in her shoulder—out of the fight, if not killed.
Ten seconds later the Blue-spot arrived, open-
mouthed. This meeting was as quick and almost as mysterious as the first. The animals
barely touched each other. The gray one
bounded aside, his head out of sight for a moment in the flash of quick movement. Spot
reeled and showed a bleeding flank. Urged
on by the men, he assaulted again, but only to
get another wound that taught him to keep off.

Now came the keeper with four more huge
Dogs. They turned these loose, and the men
armed with clubs and lassos were closing to
help in finishing the Wolf, when a small boy
came charging over the plain on a Pony. He
leaped to the ground and wriggling through
the ring flung his arms around the Wolf's neck.
He called him his "Wolfie pet," his "dear
Wolfie"—the Wolf licked his face and wagged
its tail—then the child turned on the crowd and
through his streaming tears, he—Well! it would
not do to print what he said. He was only nine,

but he was very old-fashioned, as well as a rude little boy. He had been brought up in a low saloon, and had been an apt pupil at picking up the vile talk of the place. He cursed them one and all and for generations back; he did not spare even his own father.

If a man had used such shocking and insulting language he might have been lynched, but coming from a baby, the hunters did not know what to do, so finally did the best thing. They laughed aloud—not at themselves, that is not considered good form—but they all laughed at the German whose wonderful Dogs had been worsted by a half-grown Wolf.

Jimmie now thrust his dirty, tear-stained little fist down into his very-much-of-a-boy's pocket, and from among marbles and chewing-gum, as well as tobacco, matches, pistol cartridges, and other contraband, he fished out a flimsy bit of grocer's twine and fastened it around the Wolf's neck. Then, still blubbering a little, he set out for home on the Pony, leading the Wolf and hurling a final threat and anathema at the German nobleman: "Fur two cents I 'd sic him on *you*, gol darn ye."

"His dear Wolfie."

The Winnipeg Wolf

IV

Early that winter Jimmie was taken down with a fever. The Wolf howled miserably in the yard when he missed his little friend, and finally on the boy's demand was admitted to the sick-room, and there this great wild Dog— for that is all a Wolf is—continued faithfully watching by his friend's bedside.

The fever had seemed slight at first, so that every one was shocked when there came suddenly a turn for the worse, and three days before Christmas Jimmie died. He had no more sincere mourner than his "Wolfie." The great gray creature howled in miserable answer to the church-bell tolling when he followed the body on Christmas Eve to the graveyard at St. Boniface. He soon came back to the premises behind the saloon, but when an attempt was made to chain him again, he leaped a board fence and was finally lost sight of.

Later that same winter old Renaud, the trapper, with his pretty half-breed daughter, Ninette, came to live in a little log-cabin on the river bank. He knew nothing about Jimmie Hogan, and he was not a little puzzled to find Wolf tracks and signs along the river on both sides between St. Boniface and Fort Garry. He listened with interest and doubt to tales that the Hudson Bay Company's men told of a great Gray-wolf that had come to live in the region about, and even to enter the town at night, and that was in particular attached to the woods about St. Boniface Church.

On Christmas Eve of that year when the bell tolled again as it had done for Jimmie, a lone and melancholy howling from the woods almost convinced Renaud that the stories were true. He knew the wolf-cries—the howl for help, the love song, the lonely wail, and the sharp defiance of the Wolves. This was the lonely wail.

The trapper went to the riverside and gave an answering howl. A shadowy form left the far woods and crossed on the ice to where the man sat, log-still, on a log. It came up near him, circled past and sniffed, then its eye glowed; it growled like a Dog that is a little angry, and glided back into the night.

The Winnipeg Wolf

Thus Renaud knew, and before long many townfolk began to learn, that a huge Graywolf was living in their streets, "a Wolf three times as big as the one that used to be chained at Hogan's gin-mill." He was the terror of Dogs, killing them on all possible occasions, and some said, though it was never proven, that he had devoured more than one half-breed who was out on a spree.

And this was the Winnipeg Wolf that I had seen that day in the wintry woods. I had longed to go to his help, thinking the odds so hopelessly against him, but later knowledge changed the thought. I do not know how that fight ended, but I do know that he was seen many times afterward and some of the Dogs were not.

Thus his was the strangest life that ever his kind had known. Free of all the woods and plains, he elected rather to lead a life of daily hazard in the town—each week at least some close escape, and every day a day of daring deeds; finding momentary shelter at times under the very boardwalk crossings. Hating the men and despising the Dogs, he fought his

daily way and held the hordes of Curs at bay
or slew them when he found them few or single; harried the drunkard, evaded men with
guns, learned traps—learned poison, too—just
how, we cannot tell, but learn it he did, for he
passed it again and again, or served it only
with a Wolf's contempt.

Not a street in Winnipeg that he did not
know; not a policeman in Winnipeg that had
not seen his swift and shadowy form in the
gray dawn as he passed where he would; not
a Dog in Winnipeg that did not cower and
bristle when the telltale wind brought proof
that old Garou was crouching near. His only
path was the warpath, and all the world his
foes. But throughout this lurid, semi-mythic
record there was one recurring pleasant thought
—Garou never was known to harm a child.

V

Ninette was a desert-born beauty like her
Indian mother, but gray-eyed like her Nor-
mandy father, a sweet girl of sixteen, the belle
of her set. She might have married any one

The Winnipeg Wolf

of the richest and steadiest young men of the country, but of course, in feminine perversity her heart was set on that ne'er-do-well, Paul des Roches. A handsome fellow, a good dancer and a fair violinist, Fiddler Paul was in demand at all festivities, but he was a shiftless drunkard and it was even whispered that he had a wife already in Lower Canada. Renaud very properly dismissed him when he came to urge his suit, but dismissed him in vain. Ninette, obedient in all else, would not give up her lover. The very day after her father had ordered him away she promised to meet him in the woods just across the river. It was easy to arrange this, for she was a good Catholic, and across the ice to the church was shorter than going around by the bridge. As she went through the snowy wood to the tryst she noticed that a large gray Dog was following. It seemed quite friendly, and the child (for she was still that) had no fear, but when she came to the place where Paul was waiting, the gray Dog went forward rumbling in its chest. Paul gave one look, knew it for a huge Wolf, then fled like the coward he was. He afterward said he ran for his gun. He must have forgotten where it was, as he climbed the nearest tree to find it. Meanwhile Ninette ran home across the ice to tell Paul's friends of his danger. Not finding any firearms up the tree, the valiant lover made a spear by fastening his knife to a branch and succeeded in giving Garou a painful wound on the head. The savage creature growled horribly but thenceforth kept at a safe distance, though plainly showing his intention to wait till the man came down. But the approach of a band of rescuers changed his mind, and he went away.

Fiddler Paul found it easier to explain matters to Ninette than he would to any one else. He still stood first in her affections, but so hopelessly ill with her father that they decided on an elopement, as soon as he should return from Fort Alexander, whither he was to go for the Company, as dog-driver. The Factor was very proud of his train Dogs—three great Huskies with curly, bushy tails, big and strong as Calves, but fierce and lawless as pirates. With these the Fiddler Paul was to drive to Fort Alexander from Fort Garry—the bearer of

The Winnipeg Wolf

several important packets.   He was an expert
Dog-driver, which usually means relentlessly
cruel.   He set off blithely down the river
in the morning, after the several necessary
drinks of whiskey.   He expected to be gone
a week, and would then come back with
twenty dollars in his pocket, and having thus
provided the sinews of war, would carry out
the plan of elopement.   Away they went down
the river on the ice.   The big Dogs pulled
swiftly but sulkily as he cracked the long whip
and shouted, *"Allez, allez, marchez."*   They
passed at speed by Renaud's shanty on the
bank, and Paul, cracking his whip and running
behind the train, waved his hand to Ninette
as she stood by the door.   Speedily the cariole
with the sulky Dogs and drunken driver disappeared around the bend—and that was the
last ever seen of Fiddler Paul.

'That evening the Huskies came back singly to
Fort Garry.   They were spattered with frozen
blood, and were gashed in several places.   But
strange to tell they were quite " unhungry."

Runners went on the back trail and recovered the packages.   They were lying on the

ice unharmed. Fragments of the sled were strewn for a mile or more up the river; not far from the packages were shreds of clothing that had belonged to the Fiddler.

It was quite clear, the Dogs had murdered and eaten their driver.

The Factor was terribly wrought up over the matter. It might cost him his Dogs. He refused to believe the report and set off to sift the evidence for himself. Renaud was chosen to go with him, and before they were within three miles of the fatal place Renaud pointed to a very large track crossing from the east to the west bank of the river, just after the Dog sled. He ran it backward for a mile or more on the eastern bank, noted how it had walked when the Dogs walked and run when they ran, before he turned to the Factor and said: " A beeg Voolf—he come after ze cariole all ze time."

Now they followed the track where it had crossed to the west shore. Two miles above Kildonan woods the Wolf had stopped his gallop to walk over to the sled trail, had followed it a few yards, then had returned to the woods.

The Winnipeg Wolf

"Paul he drop somesin' here, ze packet maybe; ze Voolf he come for smell. He follow so—now he know zat eez ze drunken Paul vot slash heem on ze head."

A mile farther the Wolf track came galloping on the ice behind the cariole. The man track disappeared now, for the driver had leaped on the sled and lashed the Dogs. Here is where he cut adrift the bundles. That is why things were scattered over the ice. See how the Dogs were bounding under the lash. Here was the Fiddler's knife in the snow. He must have dropped it in trying to use it on the Wolf. And here—what! the Wolf track disappears, but the sled track speeds along. The Wolf has leaped on the sled. The Dogs, in terror, added to their speed; but on the sleigh behind them there is a deed of vengeance done. In a moment it is over; both roll off the sled; the Wolf track reappears on the east side to seek the woods. The sled swerves to the west bank, where, after half a mile, it is caught and wrecked on a root.

The snow also told Renaud how the Dogs, entangled in the harness, had fought with each

other, had cut themselves loose, and trotting
homeward by various ways up the river, had
gathered at the body of their late tyrant and
devoured him at a meal.

Bad enough for the Dogs, still they were
cleared of the murder. That certainly was
done by the Wolf, and Renaud, after the shock
of horror was past, gave a sigh of relief and
added, "Eet is le Garou. He hab save my
leel girl from zat Paul. He always was good
to children."

VI

This was the cause of the great final hunt
that they fixed for Christmas Day just two years
after the scene at the grave of Little Jim. It
seemed as though all the Dogs in the country
were brought together. The three Huskies
were there—the Factor considered them essen-
tial—there were Danes and trailers and a rabble of farm Dogs and nondescripts. They
spent the morning beating all the woods east
of St. Boniface and had no success. But a telephone message came that the trail they sought
had been seen near the Assiniboine woods west

of the city, and an hour later the hunt was yelling on the hot scent of the Winnipeg Wolf.

Away they went, a rabble of Dogs, a motley rout of horsemen, a mob of men and boys on foot. Garou had no fear of the Dogs, but men he knew had guns and were dangerous. He led off for the dark timber line of the Assiniboine, but the horsemen had open country and they headed him back. He coursed along the Colony Creek hollow and so eluded the bullets already flying. He made for a barbwire fence, and passing that he got rid of the horsemen for a time, but still must keep the hollow that baffled the bullets. The Dogs were now closing on him. All he might have asked would probably have been to be left alone with them—forty or fifty to one as they were— he would have taken the odds. The Dogs were all around him now, but none dared to close in. A lanky Hound, trusting to his speed, ran alongside at length and got a side chop from Garou that laid him low. The horsemen were forced to take a distant way around, but now the chase was toward the town, and more men and Dogs came running out to join the fray.

The Winnipeg Wolf

The Wolf turned toward the slaughter-house, a familiar resort, and the shooting ceased on account of the houses, as well as the Dogs, being so near. These were indeed now close enough to encircle him and hinder all further flight. He looked for a place to guard his rear for a final stand, and seeing a wooden foot-bridge over a gutter he sprang in, there faced about and held the pack at bay. The men got bars and demolished the bridge. He leaped out, knowing now that he had to die, but ready, wishing only to make a worthy fight, and then for the first time in broad day view of all his foes he stood—the shadowy Dog-killer, the disembodied voice of St. Boniface woods, the wonderful Winnipeg Wolf.

VII

At last after three long years of fight he stood before them alone, confronting twoscore Dogs, and men with guns to back them—but facing them just as resolutely as I saw him that day in the wintry woods. The same old curl was on his lips—the hard-knit flanks heaved

The Winnipeg Wolf

just a little, but his green and yellow eye glowed steadily. The Dogs closed in, led not by the huge Huskies from the woods—they evidently knew too much for that—but by a Bulldog from the town; there was scuffling of many feet; a low rumbling for a time replaced the yapping of the pack; a flashing of those red and grizzled jaws, a momentary hurl back of the onset, and again he stood alone and braced, the grim and grand old bandit that he was. Three times they tried and suffered. Their boldest were lying about him. The first to go down was the Bulldog. Learning wisdom now, the Dogs held back, less sure; but his square-built chest showed never a sign of weakness yet, and after waiting impatiently he advanced a few steps, and thus, alas! gave to the gunners their long-expected chance. Three rifles rang, and in the snow Garou went down at last, his life of combat done.

He had made his choice. His days were short and crammed with quick events. His tale of many peaceful years was spent in three of daily brunt. He picked his trail, a new trail, high and short. He chose to drink his cup at a single gulp, and break the glass—but he left a deathless name.

Who can look into the mind of the Wolf? Who can show us his wellspring of motive? Why should he still cling to a place of endless tribulation? It could not be because he knew no other country, for the region is limitless, food is everywhere, and he was known at least as far as Selkirk. Nor could his motive be revenge. No animal will give up its whole life to seeking revenge; that evil kind of mind is found in man alone. The brute creation seeks for peace.

There is then but one remaining bond to chain him, and that the strongest claim that anything can own—the mightiest force on earth.

The Wolf is gone. The last relic of him was lost in the burning Grammar School, but to this day the sexton of St. Boniface Church avers that the tolling bell on Christmas Eve never fails to provoke that weird and melancholy Wolf-cry from the wooded graveyard a hundred steps away, where they laid his Little Jim, the only being on earth that ever met him with the touch of love.

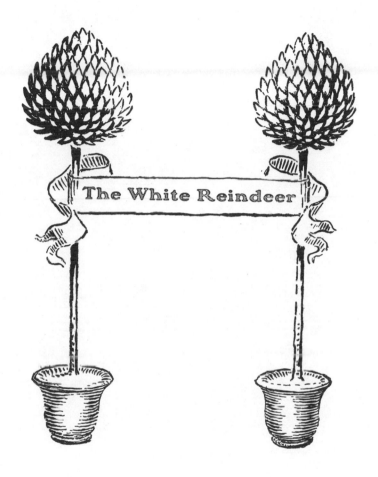

The White Reindeer

The Legend of the White Reindeer

Skoal! Skoal! For Norway Skoal!
Sing ye the song of the Vand-dam troll.
When I am hiding
Norway's luck
On a White Storbuk
Comes riding, riding.

THE SETTING

LEAK, black, deep, and cold is Utrovand, a long pocket of glacial water, a crack in the globe, a wrinkle in the high Norwegian mountains, blocked with another mountain, and flooded with a frigid flood, three thousand feet above its Mother Sea, and yet no closer to its Father Sun.

The Legend of the White Reindeer

Around its cheerless shore is a belt of stunted trees, that sends a long tail up the high valley, till it dwindles away to sticks and moss, as it also does some half-way up the granite hills that rise a thousand feet, encompassing the lake. This is the limit of trees, the end of the growth of wood. The birch and willow are the last to drop out of the long fight with frost. Their miniature thickets are noisy with the cries of Fieldfare, Pipit, and Ptarmigan, but these are left behind on nearing the upper plateau, where shade of rock and sough of wind are all that take their place. The chilly Hoifjeld rolls away, a rugged, rocky plain, with great patches of snow in all the deeper hollows, and the distance blocked by snowy peaks that rise and roll and whiter gleam, till, dim and dazzling in the north, uplifts the Jötunheim, the home of spirits, of glaciers, and of the lasting snow.

The treeless stretch is one vast attest to the force of heat. Each failure of the sun by one degree is marked by a lower realm of life. The northern slope of each hollow is less boreal than its southern side. The pine and spruce have given out long ago; the mountain-ash

324

went next; the birch and willow climbed up
half the slope. Here, nothing grows but creep-
ing plants and moss. The plain itself is pale
grayish green, one vast expanse of reindeer-
moss, but warmed at spots into orange by great
beds of polytrichum, and, in sunnier nooks,
deepened to a herbal green. The rocks that are
scattered everywhere are of a delicate lilac, but
each is variegated with spreading frill-edged
plasters of gray-green lichen or orange powder-
streaks and beauty-spots of black. These rocks
have great power to hold the heat, so that each
of them is surrounded by a little belt of heat-
loving plants that could not otherwise live so
high. Dwarfed representatives of the birch
and willow both are here, hugging the genial
rock, as an old French *habitant* hugs his stove
in winter-time, spreading their branches over it,
instead of in the frigid air. A foot away is
seen a chillier belt of heath, and farther off,
colder, where none else can grow, is the omni-
present gray-green reindeer-moss that gives its
color to the upland. The hollows are still filled
with snow, though now it is June. But each of
these white expanses is shrinking, spending it-

The Legend of the White Reindeer

self in ice-cold streams that somehow reach the lake. These *snö-fläcks* show no sign of life, not even the 'red-snow' tinge, and around each is a belt of barren earth, to testify that life and warmth can never be divorced.

Birdless and lifeless, the gray-green snow-pied waste extends over all the stretch that is here between the timber-line and the snow-line, above which winter never quits its hold. Farther north both come lower, till the timber-line is at the level of the sea; and all the land is in that treeless belt called Tundra in the Old World, and Barrens in the New, and that everywhere is the Home of the Reindeer—the Realm of the Reindeer-moss.

I

In and out it flew, in and out, over the water and under, as the Varsimlé, the leader doe of the Reindeer herd, walked past on the vernal banks, and it sang : —

" *Skoal! Skoal! Gamle Norge Skoal!* " and more about " a White Reindeer and Norway's good luck," as though the singer were gifted with special insight.

The Legend of the White Reindeer

When old Sveggum built the Vand-dam on the Lower Hoifjeld, just above the Utrovand, and set his *ribesten* a-going, he supposed that he was the owner of it all. But some one was there before him. And in and out of the spouting stream this some one dashed, and sang songs that he made up to fit the place and the time. He skipped from *skjœke* to *skjœke* of the wheel, and did many things which Sveggum could set down only to luck—whatever that is; and some said that Sveggum's luck was a Wheel-troll, a Water-fairy, with a brown coat and a white beard, one that lived on land or in water, as he pleased.

But most of Sveggum's neighbors saw only a Fossekal, the little Waterfall Bird that came each year and danced in the stream, or dived where the pool is deep. And maybe both were right, for some of the very oldest peasants will tell you that a Fairy-troll may take the form of a man or the form of a bird. Only this bird lived a life no bird can live, and sang songs that men never had sung in Norway. Wonderful vision had he, and sights he saw that man never saw. For the Fieldfare would build be-

The Legend of the White Reindeer

fore him, and the Lemming fed its brood under his very eyes. Eyes were they to see; for the dark speck on Suletind that man could barely glimpse was a Reindeer, with half-shed coat, to him; and the green slime on the Vandren was beautiful green pasture with a banquet spread.

Oh, Man is so blind, and makes himself so hated! But Fossekal harmed none, so none were afraid of him. Only he sang, and his songs were sometimes mixed with fun and prophecy, or perhaps a little scorn.

From the top of the tassel-birch he could mark the course of the Vand-dam stream past the Nystuen hamlet to lose itself in the gloomy waters of Utrovand; or by a higher flight he could see across the barren upland that rolled to Jötunheim in the north.

The great awakening was on now. The springtime had already reached the woods; the valleys were a-throb with life; new birds coming from the south, winter sleepers reappearing, and the Reindeer that had wintered in the lower woods should soon again be seen on the uplands.

Not without a fight do the Frost Giants give

The Legend of the White Reindeer

up the place so long their own; a great battle
was in progress; but the Sun was slowly, surely
winning, and driving them back to their Jötunheim. At every hollow and shady place they
made another stand, or sneaked back by night,
only to suffer another defeat. Hard hitters
these, as they are stubborn fighters; many a
granite rock was split and shattered by their
blows in reckless fight, so that its inner fleshy
tints were shown and warmly gleamed among
the gray-green rocks that dotted the plain, like
the countless flocks of Thor. More or less of
these may be found at every place of battle-
brunt, and straggled along the slope of Suletind was a host that reached for half a mile.
But stay! these moved. Not rocks were they,
but living creatures.

They drifted along erratically, yet one way,
all up the wind. They swept out of sight in a
hollow, to reappear on a ridge much nearer,
and serried there against the sky, we marked
their branching horns, and knew them for the
Reindeer in their home.

The band came drifting our way, feeding
like Sheep, grunting like only themselves. Each

one found a grazing-spot, stood there till it was cleared off, then trotted on crackling hoofs to the front in search of another. So the band was ever changing in rank and form. But one there was that was always at or near the van—a large and well-favored Simlé, or Hind. However much the band might change and spread, she was in the forefront, and the observant would soon have seen signs that she had an influence over the general movement—that she, indeed, was the leader. Even the big Bucks, in their huge velvet-clad antlers, admitted this untitular control; and if one, in a spirit of independence, evinced a disposition to lead elsewhere, he soon found himself uncomfortably alone.

The Varsimlé, or leading Hind, had kept the band hovering, for the last week or two, along the timber-line, going higher each day to the baring uplands, where the snow was clearing and the deer-flies were blown away. As the pasture zone had climbed she had followed in her daily foraging, returning to the sheltered woods at sundown, for the wild things fear the cold night wind even as man does. But now the deer-flies were rife in the woods, and the

The Legend of the White Reindeer

rocky hillside nooks warm enough for the nightly bivouac, so the woodland was deserted.

Probably the leader of a band of animals does not consciously pride itself on leadership, yet has an uncomfortable sensation when not followed. But there are times with all when solitude is sought. The Varsimlé had been fat and well through the winter, yet now was listless, and lingered with drooping head as the grazing herd moved past her.

Sometimes she stood gazing blankly while the unchewed bunch of moss hung from her mouth, then roused to go on to the front as before; but the spells of vacant stare and the hankering to be alone grew stronger. She turned downward to seek the birch woods, but the whole band turned with her. She stood stock-still, with head down. They grazed and grunted past, leaving her like a statue against the hillside. When all had gone on, she slunk quietly away; walked a few steps, looked about, made a pretense of grazing, snuffed the ground, looked after the herd, and scanned the hills; then downward fared toward the sheltering woods.

Once as she peered over a bank she sighted

The Legend of the White Reindeer

another Simlé, a doe Reindeer, uneasily wandering by itself. But the Varsimlé wished not for company. She did not know why, but she felt that she must hide away somewhere.

She stood still until the other had passed on, then turned aside, and went with faster steps and less wavering, till she came in view of Utrovand, away down by the little stream that turns old Sveggum's ribesten. Up above the dam she waded across the limpid stream, for deep-laid and sure is the instinct of a wild animal to put running water between itself and those it shuns. Then, on the farther bank, now bare and slightly green, she turned, and passing in and out among the twisted trunks, she left the noisy Vand-dam. On the higher ground beyond she paused, looked this way and that, went on a little, but returned; and here, completely shut in by softly painted rocks, and birches wearing little springtime hangers, she seemed inclined to rest; yet not to rest, for she stood uneasily this way and that, driving away the flies that settled on her legs, heeding not at all the growing grass, and thinking she was hid from all the world.

The Legend of the White Reindeer

But nothing escapes the Fossekal.   He had
seen her leave the herd, and now he sat on a
gorgeous rock that overhung, and sang as
though he had waited for this and knew that
the fate of the nation might turn on what
passed in this far glen.   He sang:

> Skoal! Skoal!   For Norway Skoal!
> Sing ye the song of the Vand-dam troll.
> When I am hiding
> Norway's luck
> On a White Storbuk
> Comes riding, riding.

There are no Storks in Norway, and yet an
hour later there was a wonderful little Reindeer
lying beside the Varsimlé.   She was brushing
his coat, licking and mothering him, proud and
happy as though this was the first little Renskalv ever born.   There might be hundreds
born in the herd that month, but probably no
more like this one, for he was snowy white,
and the song of the singer on the painted rock
was about

> Good luck, good luck,
> And a White Storbuk,

333

as though he foresaw clearly the part that the White Calf was to play when he grew to be a Storbuk.

But another wonder now came to pass. Before an hour, there was a second little Calf— a brown one this time. Strange things happen, and hard things are done when they needs must. Two hours later, when the Varsimlé led the White Calf away from the place, there was no Brown Calf, only some flattened rags with calf-hair on them.

The mother was wise: better one strongling than two weaklings. Within a few days the Simlé once more led the band, and running by her side was the White Calf. The Varsimlé considered him in all things, so that he really set the pace for the band, which suited very well all the mothers that now had Calves with them. Big, strong, and wise was the Varsimlé, in the pride of her strength, and this White Calf was the flower of her prime. He often ran ahead of his mother as she led the herd, and Rol, coming on them one day, laughed aloud at the sight as they passed, old and young, fat Simlé and antlered Storbuk, a great brown

334

The Legend of the White Reindeer

herd, all led, as it seemed, by a little White
Calf.

So they drifted away to the high mountains,
to be gone all summer. "Gone to be taught
by the spirits who dwell where the Black Loon
laughs on the ice," said Lief of the Lower
Dale; but Sveggum, who had always been
among the Reindeer, said: "Their mothers
are the teachers, even as ours are."

When the autumn came, old Sveggum saw a
moving snö-fläck far off on the brown moor-
land; but the Troll saw a white yearling, a
Nekbuk; and when they ranged alongside of
Utrovand to drink, the still sheet seemed fully
to reflect the White One, though it barely
sketched in the others, with the dark hills behind.

Many a little Calf had come that spring, and
had drifted away on the moss-barrens, to come
back no more; for some were weaklings and
some were fools; some fell by the way, for that
is law; and some would not learn the rules,
and so died. But the White Calf was strongest
of them all, and he was wise, so he learned of
his mother, who was wisest of them all. He

335

learned that the grass on the sun side of a rock is sweet, and though it looks the same in the dark hollows, it is there worthless. He learned that when his mother's hoofs crackled he must be up and moving, and when all the herd's hoofs crackled there was danger, and he must keep by his mother's side. For this crackling is like the whistling of a Whistler Duck's wings: it is to keep the kinds together. He learned that where the little Bomuldblomster hangs its cotton tufts is dangerous bog; that the harsh cackle of the Ptarmigan means that close at hand are Eagles, as dangerous for Fawn as for Bird. He learned that the little troll-berries are deadly, that when the *verra*-flies come stinging he must take refuge on a snow-patch, and that of all animal smells only that of his mother was to be fully trusted. He learned that he was growing. His flat calf sides and big joints were changing to the full barrel and clean limbs of the Yearling, and the little bumps which began to show on his head when he was only a fortnight old were now sharp, hard spikes that could win in fight.

More than once they had smelt that dreaded destroyer of the north that men call the Gjerv

336

The Legend of the White Reindeer

or Wolverene; and one day, as this danger-
scent came suddenly and in great strength, a
huge blot of dark brown sprang rumbling from
a rocky ledge, and straight for the foremost—
the White Calf. His eye caught the flash of a
whirling, shaggy mass, with gleaming teeth and
eyes, hot-breathed and ferocious. Blank horror set his hair on end; his nostrils flared in
fear: but before he fled there rose within another feeling—one of anger at the breaker of
his peace, a sense that swept all fear away,
braced his legs, and set his horns at charge.
The brown brute landed with a deep-chested
growl, to be received on the young one's spikes.
They pierced him deeply, but the shock was
overmuch; it bore the White One down, and he
might yet have been killed but that his mother,
alert and ever near, now charged the attacking
monster, and heavier, better armed, she hurled
and speared him to the ground. And the
White Calf, with a very demon glare in his once
mild eyes, charged too; and even after the
Wolverene was a mere hairy mass, and his
mother had retired to feed, he came, snorting
out his rage, to drive his spikes into the hateful

337

thing, till his snowy head was stained with his adversary's blood.

Thus he showed that below the ox-like calm exterior was the fighting beast; that he was like the men of the north, rugged, square-built, calm, slow to wrath, but when aroused "seeing red."

When they ranked together by the lake that fall, the Fossekal sang his old song:

> When I am hiding
> Norway's luck
> On a White Storbuk
> Comes riding, riding,

as though this was something he had awaited, then disappeared no one knew where. Old Sveggum had seen it flying through the stream, as birds fly through the air, walking in the bottom of a deep pond as a Ptarmigan walks on the rocks, living as no bird can live; and now the old man said it had simply gone southward for the winter. But old Sveggum could neither read nor write: how should he know?

338

The White Renskalv Facing the Wolverene.

The Legend of the White Reindeer

II

Each springtime when the Reindeer passed over Sveggum's mill-run, as they moved from the lowland woods to the bleaker shore of Utrovand, the Fossekal was there to sing about the White Storbuk, which each year became more truly the leader.

That first spring he stood little higher than a Hare. When he came to drink in the autumn, his back was above the rock where Sveggum's stream enters Utrovand. Next year he barely passed under the stunted birch, and the third year the Fossekal on the painted rock was looking up, not down, at him as he passed. This was the autumn when Rol and Sveggum sought the Hoifjeld to round up their half-wild herd and select some of the strongest for the sled. There was but one opinion about the Storbuk. Higher than the others, heavier, white as snow, with a mane that swept the shallow drifts, breasted like a Horse and with horns like a storm-grown oak, he was king of the herd, and might easily be king of the road.

The Legend of the White Reindeer

There are two kinds of deer-breakers, as there are two kinds of horse-breakers: one that tames and teaches the animal, and gets a spirited, friendly helper; one that aims to break its spirit, and gets only a sullen slave, ever ready to rebel and wreak its hate. Many a Lapp and many a Norsk has paid with his life for brutality to his Reindeer, and Rol's days were shortened by his own pulk-Ren. But Sveggum was of gentler sort. To him fell the training of the White Storbuk. It was slow, for the Buck resented all liberties from man, as he did from his brothers; but kindness, not fear, was the power that tamed him, and when he had learned to obey and glory in the sled race, it was a noble sight to see the great white mild-eyed beast striding down the long snow-stretch of Utrovand, the steam jetting from his nostrils, the snow swirling up before like the curling waves on a steamer's bow, sled, driver, and Deer all dim in flying white.

Then came the Yule-tide Fair, with the races on the ice, and Utrovand for once was gay. The sullen hills about reëchoed with merry shouting. The Reindeer races were first, with

342

The Legend of the White Reindeer

many a mad mischance for laughter. Rol
himself was there with his swiftest sled Deer, a
tall, dark, five-year-old, in his primest prime.
But over-eager, over-brutal, he harried the sullen, splendid slave till in mid-race—just when
in a way to win—it turned at a cruel blow, and
Rol took refuge under the upturned sled until
it had vented its rage against the wood; and
so he lost the race, and the winner was the
young White Storbuk. Then he won the five-
mile race around the lake; and for each triumph Sveggum hung a little silver bell on his
harness, so that now he ran and won to merry
music.

Then came the Horse races,—running races
these; the Reindeer only trots,—and when
Balder, the victor Horse, received his ribbon
and his owner the purse, came Sveggum with
all his winnings in his hand, and said: "Ho,
Lars, thine is a fine Horse, but mine is a better
Storbuk; let us put our winnings together and
race, each his beast, for all."

A Ren against a Race-horse—such a race
was never seen till now. Off at the pistol-crack
they flew. "Ho, Balder! (*cluck!*) Ho, hi,

The Legend of the White Reindeer

Balder!" Away shot the beautiful Racer, and the Storbuk, striding at a slower trot, was left behind.

"Ho, Balder!" "Hi, Storbuk!" How the people cheered as the Horse went bounding and gaining! But he had left the line at his top speed; the Storbuk's rose as he flew—faster—faster. The Pony ceased to gain. A mile whirled by; the gap began to close. The Pony had over-spurted at the start, but the Storbuk was warming to his work—striding evenly, swiftly, faster yet, as Sveggum cried in encouragement: "Ho, Storbuk! good Storbuk!" or talked to him only with a gentle rein. At the turning-point the pair were neck and neck; then the Pony—though well driven and well shod—slipped on the ice, and thenceforth held back as though in fear, so the Storbuk steamed away. The Pony and his driver were far behind when a roar from every human throat in Filefjeld told that the Storbuk had passed the wire and won the race. And yet all this was before the White Ren had reached the years of his full strength and speed.

Once that day Rol essayed to drive the

344

The Legend of the White Reindeer

Storbuk. They set off at a good pace, the White Buk ready, responsive to the single rein, and his mild eyes veiled by his drooping lashes. But, without any reason other than the habit of brutality, Rol struck him. In a moment there was a change. The Racer's speed was checked, all four legs braced forward till he stood ; the drooping lids were raised, the eyes rolled—there was a green light in them now. Three puffs of steam were jetted from each nostril. Rol shouted, then, scenting danger, quickly upset the sled and hid beneath. The Storbuk turned to charge the sled, sniffing and tossing the snow with his foot ; but little Knute, Sveggum's son, ran forward and put his arms around the Storbuk's neck ; then the fierce look left the Reindeer's eye, and he suffered the child to lead him quietly back to the starting-point. Beware, O driver ! the Reindeer, too, " sees red."

This was the coming of the White Storbuk for the folk of Filefjeld.

In the two years that followed he became famous throughout that country as Sveggum's Storbuk, and many a strange exploit was told

345

of him. In twenty minutes he could carry old Sveggum round the six-mile rim of Utrovand. When the snow-slide buried all the village of Holaker, it was the Storbuk that brought the word for help to Opdalstole and returned again over the forty miles of deep snow in seven hours, to carry brandy, food, and promise of speedy aid.

When over-venturesome young Knute Sveggumsen broke through the new thin ice of Utrovand, his cry for help brought the Storbuk to the rescue; for he was the gentlest of his kind and always ready to come at call.

He brought the drowning boy in triumph to the shore, and as they crossed the Vand-dam stream, there was the Troll-bird to sing:

> Good luck, good luck,
> With the White Storbuk.

After which he disappeared for months— doubtless dived into some subaqueous cave to feast and revel all winter; although Sveggum did not believe it was so.

The Legend of the White Reindeer

III

How often is the fate of kingdoms given into child hands, or even committed to the care of Bird or Beast! A She-wolf nursed the Roman Empire.  A Wren pecking crumbs on a drum-head aroused the Orange army, it is said, and ended the Stuart reign in Britain. Little wonder, then, that to a noble Reindeer Buk should be committed the fate of Norway: that the Troll on the wheel should have reason in his rhyme.

These were troublous times in Scandinavia. Evil men, traitors at heart, were sowing dissension between the brothers Norway and Sweden. "Down with the Union!" was becoming the popular cry.

Oh, unwise peoples! If only you could have been by Sveggum's wheel to hear the Troll when he sang:

> The Raven and the Lion
>   They held the Bear at bay;
> But he picked the bones of both
>   When they quarrelled by the way.

347

The Legend of the White Reindeer

Threats of civil war, of a fight for independence, were heard throughout Norway. Meetings were held more or less secretly, and at each of them was some one with well-filled pockets and glib tongue, to enlarge on the country's wrongs, and promise assistance from an outside irresistible power as soon as they showed that they meant to strike for freedom. No one openly named the power. That was not necessary; it was everywhere felt and understood. Men who were real patriots began to believe in it. Their country was wronged. Here was one to set her right. Men whose honor was beyond question became secret agents of this power. The state was honeycombed and mined; society was a tangle of plots. The king was helpless, though his only wish was for the people's welfare. Honest and straightforward, what could he do against this far-reaching machination? The very advisers by his side were corrupted through mistaken patriotism. The idea that they were playing into the hands of the foreigner certainly never entered into the minds of these dupes — at least, not those of the rank and file. One or two,

348

The Legend of the White Reindeer

tried, selected, and bought by the arch-enemy, knew the real object in view, and the chief of these was Borgrevinck, a former lansman of Nordlands. A man of unusual gifts, a member of the Storthing, a born leader, he might have been prime minister long ago, but for the distrust inspired by several unprincipled dealings. Soured by what he considered want of appreciation, balked in his ambition, he was a ready tool when the foreign agent sounded him. At first his patriotism had to be sopped, but that necessity disappeared as the game went on, and perhaps he alone, of the whole far-reaching conspiracy, was prepared to strike at the Union for the benefit of the foreigner.

Plans were being perfected,—army officers being secretly misled and won over by the specious talk of "their country's wrongs," and each move made Borgrevinck more surely the head of it all,—when a quarrel between himself and the "deliverer" occurred over the question of recompense. Wealth untold they were willing to furnish; but regal power, never. The quarrel became more acute. Borgrevinck continued to attend all meetings, but was ever more careful to centre all power in himself, and even prepared to turn round to the king's party if necessary to further his ambition. The betrayal of his followers would purchase his own safety. But proofs he must have, and he set about getting signatures to a declaration of rights which was simply a veiled confession of treason. Many of the leaders he had deluded into signing this before the meeting at Laersdalsoren. Here they met in the early winter, some twenty of the patriots, some of them men of position, all of them men of brains and power. Here, in the close and stifling parlor, they planned, discussed, and questioned. Great hopes were expressed, great deeds were forecast, in that stove-hot room.

Outside, against the fence, in the winter night, was a Great White Reindeer, harnessed to a sled, but lying down with his head doubled back on his side as he slept, calm, unthoughtful, ox-like. Which seemed likelier to decide the nation's fate, the earnest thinkers indoors, or the ox-like sleeper without? Which seemed more vital to Israel, the bearded council in King Saul's tent, or the light-hearted shepherd-

The Legend of the White Reindeer

boy hurling stones across the brook at Bethlehem? At Laersdalsoren it was as before: deluded by Borgrevinck's eloquent plausibility, all put their heads in the noose, their lives and country in his hands, seeing in this treacherous monster a very angel of self-sacrificing patriotism. All? No, not all. Old Sveggum was there. He could neither read nor write. That was his excuse for not signing. He could not read a letter in a book, but he could read something of the hearts of men. As the meeting broke up he whispered to Axel Tanberg: "Is his own name on that paper?" And Axel, starting at the thought, said: "No." Then said Sveggum: "I don't trust that man. They ought to know of this at Nystuen." For there was to be the really important meeting. But how to let them know was the riddle. Borgrevinck was going there at once with his fast Horses.

Sveggum's eye twinkled as he nodded toward the Storbuk, standing tied to the fence. Borgrevinck leaped into his sleigh and went off at speed, for he was a man of energy.

Sveggum took the bells from the harness,

351

The Legend of the White Reindeer

untied the Reindeer, stepped into the pulk. He swung the single rein, clucked to the Storbuk, and also turned his head toward Nystuen. The fast Horses had a long start, but before they had climbed the eastward hill Sveggum needs must slack, so as not to overtake them. He held back till they came to the turn above the woods at Maristuen ; then he quit the road, and up the river flat he sped the Buk, a farther way, but the only way to bring them there ahead.

Squeak, crack—squeak, crack—squeak, crack —at regular intervals from the great spreading snow-shoes of the Storbuk, and the steady sough of his breath was like the *Nordland* as she passes up the Hardanger Fjord. High up, on the smooth road to the left, they could hear the jingle of the horse-bells and the shouting of Borgrevinck's driver, who, under orders, was speeding hard for Nystuen.

The highway was a short road and smooth, and the river valley was long and rough; but when, in four hours, Borgrevinck got to Nystuen, there in the throng was a face that he had just left at Laersdalsoren. He appeared

The Legend of the White Reindeer

not to notice, though nothing ever escaped him.

At Nystuen none of the men would sign. Some one had warned them. This was serious; might be fatal at such a critical point. As he thought it over, his suspicions turned more and more to Sveggum, the old fool that could not write his name at Laersdalsoren. But how did he get there before himself with his speedy Horses?

There was a dance at Nystuen that night; the dance was necessary to mask the meeting; and during that Borgrevinck learned of the swift White Ren.

The Nystuen trip had failed, thanks to the speed of the White Buk. Borgrevinck must get to Bergen before word of this, or all would be lost. There was only one way, to be sure of getting there before any one else. Possibly word had already gone from Laersdalsoren. But even at that, Borgrevinck could get there and save himself, at the price of all Norway, if need be, provided he went with the White Storbuk. He would not be denied. He was not the man to give up a point, though it

353

took all the influence he could bring to bear, this time, to get old Sveggum's leave.

The Storbuk was quietly sleeping in the corral when Sveggum came to bring him. He rose leisurely, hind legs first, stretched one, then the other, curling his tail tight on his back as he did so, shook the hay from the great antlers as though they were a bunch of twigs, and slowly followed Sveggum at the end of the tight halter. He was so sleepy and slow that Borgrevinck impatiently gave him a kick, and got for response a short snort from the Buk, and from Sveggum an earnest warning, both of which were somewhat scornfully received. The tinkling bells on the harness had been replaced, but Borgrevinck wanted them removed. He wished to go in silence. Sveggum would not be left behind when his favorite Ren went forth, so he was given a seat in the horse-sleigh which was to follow, and the driver thereof received from his master a secret hint to delay.

Then, with papers on his person to death-doom a multitude of misguided men, with fiendish intentions in his heart as well as the

354

The Legend of the White Reindeer

power to carry them out, and with the fate of Norway in his hands, Borgrevinck was made secure in the sled, behind the White Storbuk, and sped at dawn on his errand of desolation.

At the word from Sveggum the White Ren set off with a couple of bounds that threw Borgrevinck back in the pulk. This angered him, but he swallowed his wrath on seeing that it left the horse-sleigh behind. He shook the line, shouted, and the Buk settled down to a long, swinging trot. His broad hoofs clicked double at every stride. His nostrils, out level, puffed steady blasts of steam in the frosty morning as he settled to his pace. The pulk's prow cut two long shears of snow, that swirled up over man and sled till all were white. And the great ox-eyes of the King Ren blazed joyously in the delight of motion, and of conquest too, as the sound of the horse-bells faded far behind.

Even masterful Borgrevinck could not but mark with pleasure the noble creature that had balked him last night and now was lending its speed to his purpose; for it was his intention to arrive hours before the horse-sleigh, if possible.

Up the rising road they sped as though downhill, and the driver's spirits rose with the exhilarating speed. The snow groaned ceaselessly under the prow of the pulk, and the frosty creaking under the hoofs of the flying Ren was like the gritting of mighty teeth. Then came the level stretch from Nystuen's hill to Dalecarl's, and as they whirled by in the early day, little Carl chanced to peep from a window, and got sight of the Great White Ren in a white pulk with a white driver, just as it is in the stories of the Giants, and clapped his hands, and cried, " Good, good!"

But his grandfather, when *he* caught a glimpse of the white wonder that went without even sound of bells, felt a cold chill in his scalp, and went back to light a candle that he kept at the window till the sun was high, for surely this was the Storbuk of Jötunheim.

But the Ren whirled on, and the driver shook the reins and thought only of Bergen. He struck the White Steed with the loose end of the rope. The Buk gave three great snorts

356

The Legend of the White Reindeer

and three great bounds, then faster went, and
as they passed by Dyrskaur, where the Giant
sits on the edge, his head was muffled in scud,
which means that a storm is coming. The
Storbuk knew it. He sniffed, and eyed the
sky with anxious look, and even slacked a
little; but Borgrevinck yelled at the speeding
beast, though going yet as none but he could
go, and struck him once, twice, and thrice, and
harder yet. So the pulk was whirled along
like a skiff in a steamer's wake; but there was
blood in the Storbuk's eye now; and Borgrevinck
was hard put to balance the sled. The miles
flashed by like roods till Sveggum's bridge appeared. The storm-wind now was blowing,
but there was the Troll. Whence came he now,
none knew, but there he was, hopping on the
keystone and singing of

> Norway's fate and Norway's luck,
> Of the hiding Troll and the riding Buk.

Down the winding highway they came,
curving inward as they swung around the corner. At the voice on the bridge the Deer
threw back his ears and slackened his pace.

357

The Legend of the White Reindeer

Borgrevinck, not knowing whence it came, struck savagely at the Ren. The red light gleamed in those ox-like eyes. He snorted in anger and shook the great horns, but he did not stop to avenge the blow. For him was a vaster vengeance still. He onward sped as before, but from that time Borgrevinck had lost all control. The one voice that the Ren would hear had been left behind. They whirled aside, off the road, before the bridge was reached. The pulk turned over, but righted itself, and Borgrevinck would have been thrown out and killed but for the straps. It was not to be so; it seemed rather as though the every curse of Norway had been gathered into the sled for a purpose. Bruised and battered, he reappeared. The Troll from the bridge leaped lightly to the Storbuk's head, and held on to the horns as he danced and sang his ancient song, and a new song, too:

> Ha! at last! Oh, lucky day,
> Norway's curse to wipe away!

Borgrevinck was terrified and furious. He struck harder at the Storbuk as he bounded

The Legend of the White Reindeer

over the rougher snow, and vainly tried to control him. He lost his head in fear. He got
out his knife, at last, to strike at the wild Buk's
hamstrings, but a blow from the hoof sent it
flying from his hand. Their speed on the road
was slow to that they now made: no longer
striding at the trot, but bounding madly, great
five-stride bounds, the wretched Borgrevinck
strapped in the sled, alone and helpless through
his own contriving, screaming, cursing, and
praying. The Storbuk with bloodshot eyes,
madly steaming, careered up the rugged ascent,
up to the broken, stormy Hoifjeld; mounting
the hills as a Petrel mounts the rollers, skimming the flats as a Fulmar skims the shore, he
followed the trail where his mother had first
led his tottering steps, up from the Vand-dam
nook. He followed the old familiar route that
he had followed for five years, where the white-
winged Rype flies aside, where the black rock
mountains, shining white, come near and block
the sky, "where the Reindeer find their mys-
terie."

On like the little snow-wreath that the storm-
wind sends dancing before the storm, on like

The Legend of the White Reindeer

a whirlwind over the shoulder of Suletind, over the knees of Torholmenbræ—the Giants that sit at the gateway. Faster than man or beast could follow, up—up—up—and on; and no one saw them go, but a Raven that swooped behind, and flew as Raven never flew, and the Troll, the same old Troll that sang by the Vand-dam, and now danced and sang between the antlers:

> Good luck, good luck for Norway
> With the White Storbuk comes riding.

Over Tvindehoug they faded like flying scud on the moorlands, on to the gloomy distance, away toward Jötunheim, the home of the Evil Spirits, the Land of the Lasting Snow. Their every sign and trail was wiped away by the drifting storm, and the end of them no man knows.

The Norse folk awoke as from a horrid nightmare. Their national ruin was averted; there were no deaths, for there were no proofs; and the talebearer's strife was ended.

The one earthly sign remaining from that

drive is the string of silver bells that Sveggum had taken from the Storbuk's neck—the victory bells, each the record of a triumph won; and when the old man came to understand, he sighed, and hung to the string a final bell, the largest of them all.

Nothing more was ever seen or heard of the creature who so nearly sold his country, or of the White Storbuk who balked him. Yet those who live near Jötunheim say that on stormy nights, when the snow is flying and the wind is raving in the woods, there sometimes passes, at frightful speed, an enormous White Reindeer with fiery eyes, drawing a snow-white pulk, in which is a screaming wretch in white, and on the head of the Deer, balancing by the horns, is a brown-clad, white-bearded Troll, bowing and grinning pleasantly at him, and singing

Of Norway's luck
And a White Storbuk —

the same, they say, as the one that with prophetic vision sang by Sveggum's Vand-dam on

361

The Legend of the White Reindeer

a bygone day when the birches wore their springtime hangers, and a great mild-eyed Varsimlé came alone, to go away with a little white Renskalv walking slowly, demurely, by her side.

The Passing of the King Ren.

ERNEST THOMPSON SETON (1860-1946), naturalist and author, was born Ernest Thompson, in South Shields, County Durham. His family emigrated to Canada when he was six, living briefly in the small town of Lindsay, Ontario, which is the setting of TWO LITTLE SAVAGES. They then moved to Toronto, where he was educated. He adopted the surname Seton, became Naturalist to the Government of Manitoba, and founded the Woodcraft Movement, which later amalgamated with the BOY SCOUTS; he was eventually appointed Chief Scout of America. He began to write ANIMAL STORIES in the 1880s and collected these in 1898 under the title WILD ANIMALS I HAVE KNOWN. His many other books on the same model include THE TRAIL OF THE SANDHILL STAG and THE BIOGRAPHY OF A GRIZZLY. His admirers have included Richard Adams, who acknowledges the influence of his books upon WATERSHIP DOWN.